Budding Star

www.angelsunlimited.co.uk

Budding Star

ANNIE DALTON

Collins

An imprint of HarperCollins*Publishers*

For Maria, who solved several crucial problems with one flash of inspiration; Terry Hong, whose expertise and insights helped to give this story its final shape; and Miryam Sas, for her well-timed words of encouragement.

First published in Great Britain by HarperCollins*Children'sBooks* 2004
HarperCollins*Children'sBooks* is an imprint of HarperCollins*Publishers* Ltd,
77-85 Fulham Palace Road, Hammersmith,
London W6 8JB

1 3 5 7 9 8 6 4 2

The HarperCollins*Children'sBooks* website address is
www.harpercollinschildrensbooks.co.uk

ISBN 0 00 712990 4

Printed and bound in England by
Clays Ltd, St Ives plc

CHAPTER ONE

One sunny morning, a few hours after my thirteenth birthday, I totally amazed myself by unexpectedly becoming an angel.

This was not a career option I'd seriously considered to be honest. I'd been thinking more along the lines of "TV presenter". OK, strictly speaking, I'd have preferred "girl hip-hop artist", but one of my mates played my voice back when we were messing around with her sound system one time, and I sounded *exactly* like a tiny cartoon animal!

Like most of my mates, I had this idea that the sole purpose of human existence was to get myself on telly. But if I couldn't even *sing*...

After stamping around like a drama queen for a few days, I decided I'd have to break into show biz some other way. Maybe I'd be one of those cute teen celebs who get paid squillions on the basis of their warm bubbly personalities?

This probably sounds v. v. shallow, but like I said, I hadn't realised the teenage angel option was available. Even if I *had* known, the all-important entry qualification (i.e. being completely and utterly dead) would have definitely put me off.

Back then, you see, I believed that when you died, you lost absolutely everything that made you "you". So when the speeding Ford Fiesta knocked me down, that sunny summer morning, and I found myself in the Afterlife, very much in one piece, I went into pure shock!

I'm like, "You mean I get to live for EVER!! Are you SERIOUS!"

At first my new existence felt completely unreal. Everything seemed super-sparkly and *humongously* intense. I don't think there was one single moment when anything was just ordinary.

I'd wake in my tiny dorm room at the Angel Academy and I'd have to rush to the window to see if Heaven was still there!

The view blew me away every time. I'd never even *seen* fifty per cent of these colours back when I was human. I'd never seen strange futuristic skyscrapers, either, soaring up into fluffy white clouds, or a city that shimmered softly with its own mysterious inner light.

What I *totally* couldn't seem to get my head round, was that *I'd* been touched with this same special heavenly shimmer-dust.

I'd catch sight of myself in the mirror and just gaze at my reflection in absolute awe. Was that REALLY me? This was the girl I'd secretly longed to be back on Earth. Now, for reasons I didn't completely comprehend, she'd shown up in Heaven! A cool vibey Mel Beeby to fit my cool vibey environment.

You know those feel-good fantasy series they put out on TV? The kind you just have to drop everything to see. The opening credits flash up and something inside you goes, "Yess! This is how life's *supposed* to be!" Well, the Heavenly City is like that, except it's real.

The school campus I had to cross each morning on my way to class was not just some fake movie set. I could sit down on real grass, mash real daisy stems with my fingernail and make a real live heavenly daisy chain! The teenagers milling around in their cool casuals were not hired extras, but genuine angel trainees. And the dark-haired girl in jeans and cowboy boots racing towards me, waving madly, *definitely* wasn't a made-up character! Lola Sanchez was my real, and totally crazy, best friend.

It's a bizarre thought that if Lollie and I hadn't both died at such a tender age, we probably wouldn't have met. Though we have the same mad sense of humour, and almost identical taste in clothes and music, my soul-mate originally hailed from a vibey Third World city exactly one hundred years in my future! Like our teachers say, the Agency moves in SUCH mysterious ways.

The Agency is what we call the massive angelic operation, which keeps the Universe humming smoothly twenty-four-seven. There's a zillion-plus Light Agencies, if you want to get technical. But since they're all working towards the same aims, (universal peace, blah blah) everyone refers to them as "the Agency". Most kids from my school end up working for them after they graduate.

Lola and I had our sights set on being actual celestial agents, along with Reuben, our other big

b...
ange...
Planet Ea...

I think it's...
much about mak...
he actually grew...
environment of Heaven. ...
he thought everywhere was lik...
foot on Earth before he met me an...

Isn't that mind-bending!! Three teen...ers from drastically different cosmic backgrounds, studying in the same school by day, and bopping to the same heavenly hip-hop grooves by night; as if stuff like life, death, time and space had no influence over our individual destinies whatsoever!

I wish I'd known this kind of thing was possible when I was human. Maybe I wouldn't have spent so much of my time fighting Mum and Des for the remote, feeling deeply grumpy because I'd never be as rich, famous or fabulously good-looking as the kids on TV. But I truly *never* imagined the cosmos was this amazing!

What I also never imagined was the pressure. Kids like me, who get into the Academy on cosmic

pressure. We
 deep end with all the
 everyone expects us to get on

achers just go, "Yes, dear, I know you got
 injured in a train crash / hit by a stray bullet /
ocked down by a joyrider or whatever your sad
story is, and had to leave your heartbroken families
behind, but would you mind just packing your flight
bag and running down to Terminal Twenty-two?
There's a major crisis in ancient Wherever."

But you weren't going to hear me complaining.
I'd been enrolled in a fast-track angel-training
programme, at the most fabulous school in the
Universe. Me! The girl who once sat in the back of
the class, flicking through OK magazine and
gossiping about the cool characters in Buffy.

This was my chance for a fresh start and I knew
it. So instead of running around the school in my
underwear, tearing out large chunks of my own
hair, going, "Aargh! I'm dead. I'm dead!!" I packed
a few girly essentials in my bag, threw on my
pristine new combats, laced up my funky boots,
and bravely set off to ancient Wherever with the
rest of the guys.

This way of life began to feel almost normal. I got used to carrying a beeper, so the Agency could reach me any hour of the day or night. I got used to hanging out in historical hot spots, wearing the same filthy clothes for days, and living on angel trail mix. OK, I never quite got used to the trail mix. I ate it though.

It got so I couldn't imagine *not* being in the angel biz. I wanted to do this fabulously rewarding job for always and always...

And then, quite suddenly, I didn't.

OK, so it wasn't entirely sudden. Even by angelic standards, I'd been pushing it. I'd been on seven tough missions in a row, including an absolutely epic assignment to ancient Rome, where among other things, I got my heart well and truly broken. I can say that now. At the time there was so much going on I hardly noticed.

My next mission had to be the most harrowing assignment ever. Brice, this weird boy we know, had come back to school after a long spell as a cosmic dropout. Anyway, he got it into his head that if he won a HALO, people at school would finally get off his case. I should probably explain that Lola has a *leetle* thing for Brice, and I'm becoming strangely fond of him myself, so we let him sweet-talk us into submitting a joint entry.

I arrived in seventeenth-century Jamaica a few hours after my mates, to find a full-scale hurricane blowing. Unfortunately, by the time I finally caught up with my buddies, they were suffering from drastic cosmic amnesia. They didn't remember they were on a mission. They didn't remember they were angels. More disturbingly, my soul-mate Lola didn't know me from – well, she just didn't know me.

Hey, I'm a professional. I coped! We actually won a HALO, for teamwork "under unusually adverse cosmic conditions". Brice is still in shock to this day! Big happy ending all round! And it was, or it would have been. Except for the dreams.

The nightmares started as soon as I got back from the mission, and after that they came every single night without fail. The plot lines were pretty samey. Basically, I was on a mission to rescue my little sister Jade from faceless evil beings who'd overrun my planet since my death. I'd shoot awake in a cold sweat, literally screaming.

Did I run to my school counsellor and tell her about my disturbing experiences? Yeah, right! That would have been admitting I couldn't cope. I just told myself dreams didn't count. Dreams weren't real. Anyway, they're private. Only you, the dreamer, knows about them. It's almost like nothing happened, right?

My panic attack was not private sadly. Short of putting up posters and hiring an actual stadium, it couldn't have been more public if I'd tried.

It took place in front of, ooh, let me see: my entire history class (except for Reuben who was away on a trip), four guys from the maintenance crew, two dishy young time technicians, thirty primary school children who happened to be visiting Angel HQ, plus their teachers obviously.

Oh, and Fern, one of the junior agents. I think Fern was born grown-up. She's still really young, but she wears smart little suits and v. high heels, and you never saw her smile, just as you never saw her without her Agency clipboard. (Lola reckons she sleeps with it under her pillow.) Well, she was there. I think that about covers it.

This might sound strange, but my public freak-out took me completely by surprise. Despite the queasy sensations in my gut area every time I so much as thought about leaving Heaven, I believed I was fine. I believed this up to the moment we had to walk into the time portal and go whizzing off to— It really doesn't matter where, because I never actually got there. My heart started pounding as if it was going to explode. My vision blurred, and my ears felt as if my head was being forcibly held underwater.

I was breathing in huge frantic gasps, yet I couldn't seem to suck in enough oxygen. Then I simply bolted, but backwards, like a panicky baby elephant; reversing blindly past engineers and bewildered school children, leaving my classmates in shock.

Lola came rushing after me. "What's wrong, *carita*? Are you ill?"

"Maybe," I whimpered. "I don't know."

"Are you having one of your big bad premonitions?"

"I don't know." And I burst out crying.

My friend tried to calm me down, saying all trainees had wobbles sometimes, and would it help if she sang our special theme tune, but that just made me completely hysterical.

Lola didn't know what to do with me. "Why isn't Reubs here?" she muttered. "He sure picked his moment to go on a tiger-watching trip."

Mr Allbright came over looking concerned. "Is there a problem?"

"I can't do it," I choked. "I can't go in that portal."

He gave me a searching look. "Been having bad dreams? Cold sweats? Upset stomach?"

I nodded dumbly.

"You're obviously in no condition to go time-travelling. I'm sure Fern won't mind taking you back to school."

Lola wanted to stay behind to make sure I was OK, but Mr Allbright said I probably just needed a rest. So they all went off without me.

Fern drove me back to school in an Agency car. I was sure she was secretly disgusted with me. She was just too professional to let it show.

We pulled up outside my dorm. Before I could get out, she did this nervous cough. "I'm not a medic," she said in her cool grown-up voice, "but I'm fairly sure what you had just then was a cosmic panic attack."

It sounded awful, but I had to admit "cosmic panic attack" pretty much described the experience.

"You've really got two choices," she said in the same businesslike voice. "You can face your fears, or you might just want to reconsider your future career. Some people simply aren't cut out for this kind of work."

That morning Fern was wearing her silky hair pinned in a French pleat. It made her look like a perfect little Agency doll. I just knew Fern had never had a cosmic panic attack in her life.

I spent the next hour in my room, face down on my bed.

Fern's voice kept replaying in my head. Some people just aren't cut out for this kind of work. Some people just aren't... Some people...

I HAD to be an agent. If I wasn't an agent, what would I be?

I buried my face in the woolly blue bear Reuben won for me at the fair, and cried. I was crying so hard, I didn't hear the small *click,* as my stereo switched itself on.

Soon after I arrived in Heaven, Reuben burned me a copy of a song he'd written, and which eventually became our private theme tune. I must have heard it a zillion times and I still find it uplifting. Reuben doesn't have a bad voice and Lola literally sings like an angel. At one point she and Reuben sing this spine tingling harmony. It doesn't matter how down I feel, the instant I hear those feel-good opening chords, I know I can make it.

"You're not alone, you're not alone!"

I hadn't so much as breathed on my stereo, yet my friends' voices were suddenly filling the room.

I sat up, totally confused, in time to see a ball of buttercup-yellow light float in through my window.

Chapter Two

I'm going to let you in on some crucial cosmic info.

Any time you call for help, the Universe sends an answer.

This is like a LAW, OK? The Universe can't NOT answer. Sometimes you don't even have to call, the Universe answers anyway. Like now.

The glowing light ball was the colour of pure sunshine. As I watched, it morphed into a 3-D image of my buddy Reuben.

I sat open-mouthed, tears and snot mingling unattractively on my face, as he began to mime, rather awkwardly, to his own tune.

His dancing style is generally more laid-back, but

then he'd probably never sent an angelgram before. Even baby angels are taught to beam vibes to someone who needs help. But it takes YEARS of training to transmit your own personal energy, the way Reuben was doing now; and we'd had exactly one half-hour lesson with Mr Allbright. So it wasn't surprising Reubs was having a few problems mastering the technique.

Periodically, I could see right through him to the tropical foliage and flowers in the background. Plus I was getting all these atmospheric rain forest sound FX. Reuben himself was kind of staticky, like a TV channel that isn't properly tuned in. But I could make out his baby dreadlocks and cut-offs. I could actually read the cheesy message on that washed-out old T-shirt he wears, which says, **Love is the Answer**.

Part way through the track, Reuben started trying to tell me something. I kept saying, "What? Talk louder! You're breaking up!"

Finally, his voice reached me through a whoosh of static.

"Hang on in there, Beeby! I'll see you tonight."

He'd gone, taking the flutey rain-forest bird calls with him. But I felt SO much better, I can't tell you.

Not only had my angel buddy heard my silent call for help, he'd made the most massive effort to let me know he cared.

I couldn't imagine how he'd got permission to come back to school halfway through his tiger-watching trip, and I didn't care. Now I just had to find some way of getting through the day.

If I stayed up in my room brooding, I'd just get morbid, so I splashed some water on my face, whacked on some lip gloss, grabbed my jacket and headed down to the local nursery school.

When I arrived they were all excitedly raiding the dressing-up box for bear suits and fairy costumes and whatever. My normal day for helping is Wednesday, but Miss Dove seemed genuinely delighted to see me.

"I could do with an extra hand," she beamed. "They're a little overexcited today, as you can see!"

At lunch time, the preschoolers took their trays over to small brightly painted tables, and sat munching happily with their friends.

Miss Dove and I had our lunch at an adult-sized table, with a tablecloth and real glasses instead of beakers. We could hear the little angels giggling naughtily over the unfunny jokes preschoolers find so hilarious. We chatted about this and that, then she almost made me choke on my salad.

"I've told you this before, Melanie, but I make no apology for telling you again. You're a natural with this age group. You'd make the most wonderful nursery teacher. I know you've set your heart on being an agent, but if you ever change your mind—" Miss Dove's voice changed tone abruptly. "Bluebell, Lulu, I'd like you to come back now. You're *not* supposed to dematerialise without permission."

Can you believe Miss Dove wasn't even *looking*! Her excellent teacher's radar had warned her that some pupils were misbehaving.

"I'm going to count to five and I want to see you both sitting nicely at the table," she said firmly. "One, two—"

Two embarrassed little girls reappeared, very red in the face.

I was grateful to Bluebell and Lulu for providing a distraction. I had had the most disturbing thought. Suppose the Universe didn't *want* me to be a trouble-shooter, constantly putting myself in danger? Suppose it would actually *prefer* me to be a nursery teacher?

I'd been really upset when Fern suggested I might not be cut out to work in the field. Now suddenly, I felt a rush of pure longing. Life would be so simple if I took Miss Dove's advice; simple, but still really fulfilling. I'd spend my days surrounded by innocent paintings of smiley suns and lollipop trees, teaching the mysteries of the Universe through sand and water play. I'd never even have to leave Heaven, if I didn't want to.

After lunch, we took the class outside into the garden. I handed out tubs of bubble mixture while Miss Dove explained in terms her pupils could understand, that everything in the Universe was pure energy.

"Energy loves to play just like you," she told them in her special nursery teacher voice. "It likes to dress up and play at being stars and trees and birds."

"And bears," said Maudie solemnly. "It likes to dress up as bears, doesn't it?" She was still wearing her fluffy bear suit from this morning.

"That's right, Maudie! Clever girl!" said Miss Dove. "Now I want you all to take the lids off your bubbles *very* carefully. See if you can do it with no spilling. That's wonderful! Well done everyone. Let's see if you can blow some really beautiful bubbles."

In seconds, the air was crowded with gorgeous rainbow bubbles.

All the preschoolers were squealing, jumping up and down, trying to capture them. Then Lulu let out a little anguished cry.

"Now what just happened to your beautiful bubble, Lulu?" Miss Dove asked as if she didn't know.

"It poptid," she explained sadly. "It poptid right in my eye."

Maudie's beautiful bubble was next to pop. "Where did it go?" she wept. "That's what I don't know."

"Don't cry," said Obi.

I *adore* Obi. He has no hair and almost no eyebrows and he looks exactly like a three-year-old buddha!

"They didn't go away, they only changed," he explained to the tearful little girls. "They changed back to *not* being bubbles."

Maudie's face lit up. "*I* know! They've *been* bubbles and now they just want to play something else!"

I'm always telling Lola the things these babies say and she's like, "I can't *believe* four year olds can be so wise!"

OK, so Miss Dove's job wasn't what you'd call glamorous. She wasn't taking scary risks on the cosmic front line, like actual agents. But how I looked at it, she was actually teaching the celestial agents of the future – which to my mind was equally, if not MORE, important. I realised I was genuinely considering Miss Dove's suggestion. *Why not?* I asked myself defensively. It's not like I'd be letting anyone down. I'd still be working for the Light Agencies. I'd be doing it from home, that's all.

After school had finished, I walked back to my dorm. I'd just stopped in the hall to check my post, when Fern burst through the door.

"There you are," she said with relief. "I've been looking for you all afternoon. Melanie, I'm having SUCH a stressful day, and I was hoping you'd help me out?"

Fern did look unusually harassed. Her perfect French pleat had actually sprung several untidy little wisps. "I've spent the last month trying to organise a soul-retrieval weekend," she explained. "Now two trainees have dropped out right at the last minute. Do you think you'd be interested at all?"

"Probably not," I said cautiously. I had NO idea what soul-retrieval was, but I wasn't letting Fern know that.

"Are you sure?" she asked in a pleading voice. "It's going to be a fascinating course. Rose Hall is so beautiful. And Michael persuaded Jessica Lightpath to run the sessions, and as you know, Jessica hardly ever teaches trainees now." Fern beamed at me hopefully.

I'd never heard of Jessica Lightpath, but I just knew she wore woolly sweaters with rainbows on, plus she probably meditated with crystals big time.

"Gosh, love to help you out," I said, crossing my fingers behind my back, "but my friend's been away and he's coming back tonight."

Fern consulted her clipboard. "Would that be Reuben Bird?"

I gawped at her. "That's amazing! How did you know?"

"Because one of my colleagues has gone to drive him to Rose Hall."

"Reuben's going on this course!"

"Oh, yes," said Fern. "Didn't he tell you?"

I mentally replayed Reuben's angelgram.

Hang on in there, Beeby! I'll see you tonight.

I almost laughed. That boy is something else! How could he know I was going to be on a soul-retrieval course, when I hadn't even *heard* of soul-retrieval until two minutes ago!!

"So will you come?" Fern persisted.

Ever get those days when you literally feel the Universe ganging up on you from every side? Take my advice. Just give in, you'll save yourself no end of hassle!

I gave a resigned sigh. "OK. Count me in."

It had to be more fun than hanging around the dorm by myself.

Fern allowed herself a cool little smile. "I'm sure you won't regret it." She sneaked a peek at her watch. "Mel, I hate to pressure you, but you might want to run and pack. The bus is leaving in an hour."

Our teachers are constantly telling us we have to go with the flow. But I reckon an archangel would be left dizzy by a day that included a cosmic panic attack, an unscheduled angelgram AND a complete change of career direction, then wound up in a crowded minibus, swooping around bends so sharp, that if you saw them drawn on a map they'd look exactly like someone's intestines.

The atmosphere in the bus was not particularly friendly, I have to say. My fellow students on the course turned out to be from some celestial college I'd never heard of. Everyone at my school dresses in casuals. But these kids were like, *pure* boho. One girl was wearing an old-fashioned silk petticoat down to her ankles, little beaded slippers and a fringy silk shawl. Even the boys were dressed up in vintage gear. One wore what looked like a World War Two flying jacket. Another extremely good-looking boy had draped himself in one of those v. dramatic long coats I associate with vampires on TV. His name was something like "Indigo".

I love that arty boho look, don't get me wrong. It was the kids who got up my nose. They ignored me for ages, showing off tediously amongst themselves about some play they were involved in.

At last the vampire-coat boy deigned to notice me. "I don't think I saw you on Soul-Retrieval for Beginners, did I?" He had a lovely actor's voice.

I attempted a smile. "Actually this is the first one I've been to."

"Residentials are usually for intermediate students," he said in a disapproving tone.

Thanks for nothing, Fern.

"They really just asked me to make the numbers up," I explained.

"Well, I hope you can keep up," he said in a doubtful voice.

"We're SO lucky to get Jessica," gushed a girl wearing what looked like a milkmaid's smock. "What she doesn't know about DS and SR just isn't worth knowing."

The boy in the flying jacket threw me a pitying look. "DS is—"

"I DO know about Dark Studies, thanks," I said quickly.

They all exchanged glances, like, "Woo, has *she* got a chip!"

I slid down in my seat. This was going to be a *really* long weekend.

The bus turned off the main road and went bumping down a track. After a few minutes of jolting along in the ruts, periodically banging our heads on the roof, we came to a rambling country house.

Fern had told me that Rose Hall is used purely for soul-retrieval courses. Maybe that explains its truly amazing atmosphere. It feels like, centuries ago, someone struck a heavenly tuning fork and its pure and lovely vibe is still chiming on and on.

We all went to freshen up after the journey (we didn't have to share rooms, thank goodness), then came back down to dinner. I got a bit lost actually. That house is a total maze.

A delicious buffet had been left out for us. There must have been staff behind the scenes, preparing food and keeping everything pristine, but we never once saw them. It felt a bit like being looked after by friendly, but very shy, elves!

We were still eating when Reuben rolled up, lugging his ancient rucksack. A few days of living in the open had turned his skin the warm goldy colour of cinnamon toast.

I was so relieved to see him I just threw my arms around him.

He solemnly presented me with an enormous tropical flower. "It's a bit stinky," he said apologetically. "You don't notice it in the rain forest."

It was extremely stinky, but the gesture really touched me.

"Thanks, Sweetpea."

"Did you get my message?" he asked in a low voice.

I was still gazing at the flower. It was beautiful just so long as you didn't inhale. "Yeah, v. impressive transmitting skills," I whispered. "But how ever did you *know*?"

"I was sitting in a tree, watching the sun come up over a water hole, and I just got the feeling you were having a rough time."

"Only my most humiliating moment ever. I lost it totally."

Indigo was getting miffed at not being the centre of attention. He read out the message on Reub's T-shirt in his actor's voice.

"We all know love is the *answer*," he smirked. "But what, exactly, is the question?"

Reuben gave him the mischievous smile that lets you see just what he must have been like as a little angel kid. "Doesn't matter, mate. The answer's always the same."

"You might want to grab some of this food before it disappears," I suggested hastily.

The minute Reuben went off to fill his plate, the girls decided to introduce themselves! My buddy had made a bit of an impression. They all wanted to know if "Sweetpea" was his real name!

I explained that Lola originally called him Sweetpea as a private joke and now it had stuck. "Lola's always making up mad names for her mates. I'm 'Boo', I don't know why," I giggled.

Tanya (that was the petticoat girl) was totally starry-eyed. "It REALLY suits him," she sighed. "The way he gave you that flower; I've never seen anything so romantic."

I almost laughed. *Romantic? Reuben?*

But I'm really proud of Reubs, so I boasted, "He uses Sweetpea as his DJ name now."

"He does *deejaying*," gasped Tanya. "I bet he's good, isn't he?"

"Unbelievable," I said truthfully. "He does gigs on the beach most weekends. You should come and check him out."

She gave me a sideways look. "So are you and he...?"

This time I laughed outright. "No WAY! Reubs is just my mate."

My buddy strolled back, munching happily, "Has Jess arrived yet?"

Everyone's mouths fell open.

"You *know* Jessica Lightfoot?" breathed the milkmaid girl.

"We used to train at the same dojo." He chuckled. "Man, she might be old, but can she fight!"

It was like someone had flipped a switch. From being outsiders and newbies, we were suddenly the stars.

Next morning, I dragged on some jeans, threw on a T-shirt that said SOCIAL BUTTERFLY (mostly to annoy Indigo!), and went down to join the others.

Can you believe Indigo even wore his coat at breakfast!

"Do you think he *sleeps* in it?" I whispered to Reubs.

"Yeah, in a lead-lined coffin!" he whispered back.

Indigo was being v. v. charming this morning, giving me a special smile every time he passed me the marmalade, inquiring what I did at weekends and if I'd been to FEATHERS, a new club that had recently opened up.

Reuben whispered, "Think he fancies you."

I went pink. "Don't be stupid."

"Don't pretend you haven't noticed! You've got that little smirk!"

We quickly disposed of the continental breakfast laid on by the Rose Hall elves, then made our way to the lecture theatre.

Like everything else at Rose Hall it was simple and old-fashioned, with polished oak panelling and rows of plain wooden benches. The benches had also been polished to a high shine, and I immediately slid straight off! At that moment Jessica Lightpath walked into the lecture theatre.

Have you ever met anyone who literally makes the air shimmer?

Jessica's hair must originally have been jet black; now it was streaked with pure white, and twisted into a smooth knot on the back of her neck. She wore a dazzling white shirt, blue jeans and pristine white trainers; also masses of turquoise jewellery, making me wonder if she'd been Native American in a past life.

Reuben reckons Jessica has "long-distance eyes". And I know what he means. They're pure and clear, like they're seeing people and places no one else has ever seen.

Jessica started by explaining that souls usually "lose" themselves after death, for one of two reasons. "The human may have experienced terrible trauma – war, natural disaster, a plane crash – and be temporarily confused. Just occasionally souls get lost for their own evolutionary purposes."

I felt v. sophisticated, sitting in a grown-up

lecture theatre, furiously scribbling down phrases like "evolutionary purposes"!

There was something magic about that weekend. Like, the third or fourth time Jessica mentioned human souls, a tiny blue butterfly flew in through the open window!

I continued jotting down the Ten Key Points of Soul-Retrieval (or however many there were), but I could still feel the butterfly fluttering around the room, almost like I was tracking it with my nerve endings.

I felt a touch, light as a flower petal, as the butterfly settled on my wrist, and perched there, gently fanning its wings.

Jessica saw I was a bit surprised. "Butterflies are strongly attracted to soul work," she explained.

Indigo flashed me his intense smile. "This one seems quite attracted to Melanie!"

"Smoothie," Reubs muttered.

Jessica quickly got everyone back on track. "How many of you go dancing?" she asked.

People nervously put up their hands, wondering what this had to do with soul-retrieval.

"Ah, but how many of you really *love* to dance? All of you? Wonderful! So you all understand that you can only dance well, when you let yourself feel the music?"

"Yeah, of course," everyone agreed.

We angels tend to be a dancey lot!

"Soul-retrieval is the same," Jessica explained. "Everything in the Universe has its own note, its own song. We must attune ourselves to the music of this lost soul until we literally feel it inside our own hearts. Then, no matter where the soul goes, we will follow. We won't have to think. It will come quite naturally."

She swooped on Reuben and literally pulled him out of his seat. "You are the soul," she announced. "You try to surprise me and I'll do my best to follow."

Everyone went weak with relief that she hadn't picked on them. But that kind of thing doesn't bother Reubs. They began to improvise a surprisingly sexy little tango. Reuben was easily able to catch Jessica out at first, but as the dance went on, she began anticipating his moves so accurately it was uncanny. Suddenly it didn't seem like two people dancing, there was just this one thing – this beautiful breathtaking dance.

"Thank you, take a bow!" Jessica told him.

Reuben came back to his seat, grinning. Everyone clapped and cheered.

"A good dancer must be sensitive both to the music and to his or her partner!" smiled Jessica. "It's the same with soul-retrieval. In this beautiful, and sometimes dangerous cosmic dance, the soul leads and we follow. If the soul strays into a Limbo dimension, we follow. If the soul is badly confused and accidentally wanders into the Hell dimensions…"

Jessica cupped her ear expectantly.

"We follow!" we all chorused.

"Is she *serious*?" one girl whispered. "We'd have to follow it into the Hell dimensions? Don't they have specialists for that?"

Jessica seemed to be controlling her temper. "Yes they do! That's why the Agency runs these courses, to train you all to do this difficult and demanding work."

"Sorry, I wasn't thinking," the girl said humbly.

"You are new to soul-retrieval, my dear, so I will make allowances. This subject can be alarming at first."

If you ask me, Jessica is v. alarming herself, I told my new best friend, the butterfly; but I wasn't silly enough to say this aloud.

"For convenience agents use the term 'lost soul'," Jessica went on. "In reality, human souls never cease to be under Agency protection. But even though we know the happiness that awaits this confused soul in the Afterlife, we cannot force it to come with us. And so we play a patient waiting game. We wait, we watch, we follow, and we never cease to surround this soul with uplifting vibrations!"

"Sounds really boring," muttered the flying-jacket boy.

"Let me remind you that we're talking about saving an immortal soul. Our feelings really don't come into it." Jessica shot him a sharp look. "You understand that being permitted to do this work is an *honour*!"

"Yes," he said hastily. "I realise that."

Jessica fixed us with her scary long-distance eyes. "If all goes well, you will experience that miraculous moment when the soul accepts your help, and *of its own free will*, decides to move on to the next stage of existence."

She went to stand by a door that I totally hadn't noticed until now. "And now for the fun part of the course," she smiled. "Behind this door is a simulation chamber designed to replicate the type of conditions you can expect to find in Limbo dimensions!"

Promise not to laugh, but when I first got here, I thought "limbo" was the name of that embarrassing dance my step-dad tried to do one Christmas when he'd had a few too many Bacardi Breezers!!

I couldn't understand *why* our teachers kept banging on about it! Then I flicked to the back of the Angel Handbook and discovered that "limbo" is also the name of the cosmic no-man's-land that exists between the human world of Time and Space and the shimmery light fields of the Afterlife.

I can't stand angels who talk shop, so I'm not going to burble on about our experiences at Rose Hall. But I will just say that Jessica Lightpath is a truly inspiring teacher. Which is exactly what Tanya said when she presented her with a big bunch of flowers at the end of the course. Jessica actually had tears in her eyes.

I felt quite emotional myself. After a weekend playing "agents and souls", I'd become really close to everyone on the course in a way that's hard to explain. When I first became an angel trainee, working in a team was a huge challenge; now it was the thing about my work I loved the most. And I was on the verge of giving it all up to teach baby angels.

Going home on the bus, everyone was exchanging phone numbers. Indigo leaned over my seat, and gave me his special smile. "How does it feel to be the class butterfly magnet, Melanie?"

I tried to smile back. "Makes it quite tricky to take notes."

"I can lend you mine," he offered. "If you want to write it up."

"Oh, thanks. Actually, I don't know if—"

"You can copy my notes," Reuben said in my ear. "If you can read my spidery handwriting."

"Thanks, Sweetpea," I said, feeling like a lying monster.

I still hadn't told my buddy I was planning to change my career. I pretended it was because the SR course had been so full-on, but I was really just being a wuss.

On the drive home, I felt more confused than ever. Don't get me wrong, I still thought teaching baby angels was a worthwhile career. I just couldn't help thinking it might be a *teensy* bit samey, when you had to do it day after day after day. How was I going to feel, *really*, when the highlight of my week was teaching baby angels the actions to "Five Fat Sausages"?

I stared out of the window at the heavenly starscape flashing past. I remembered how I'd felt when I walked into the portal, like I couldn't breathe. I told myself there was nothing to be ashamed of. What was so cool about constantly exposing yourself to the Powers of Darkness; what was so wonderful about taking hideous cosmic risks?

I was getting that hot-potato feeling in my chest, a sign Helix is getting twitchy. Helix is what I call my inner angel. In the past, she's given me heaps of helpful angelic info, and the Mel Beeby part of me has often benefited from her wit and wisdom.

However, at this moment, I had no intention of asking for Helix's advice, because it would almost certainly contain really ugly keywords like "PODS", "SCARED", "WUSS" and "FIGHT BACK".

As in, "Admit it, babe, you're SCARED. It finally hit you that the PODS want to destroy every celestial agent in existence, and you're too much of a WUSS to face up to them and FIGHT BACK."

I shut my eyes, trying to stop tears leaking from under my lashes. Mel Beeby, I thought miserably, you are one crazy mixed-up angel.

CHAPTER THREE

"Careful what you ask for... the Universe is listening," Miss Dove constantly warns her class.

This has to be true, because let me tell you, after I came back from the soul-retrieval course I got EXACTLY what I'd been asking for.

No dangerous field trips, no urgent midnight summons from the Agency. Everything trundled along as smoothly as my nan's tea trolley. I went to school and did my assignments. I helped out at the nursery. I had a LOT of early nights.

Oh, and one time Lola and I went shopping.

Actually that was weird. I almost bought heaps of things. Like, I *almost* bought a bag. Ohh, heavenly bags are just divine. This one had a really subtle camouflage design, but was way more girly than that sounds. Inside were all these cool little pockets, making it ideal for field trips.

Then I remembered there wouldn't be any more field trips, and quickly put the bag back on the display.

Know what I bought in the end? One measly CD! When I got it back to my room, the guy had given me a CD of traditional Japanese harp music by mistake!

The Universe was setting me up, big time, but I didn't notice.

I felt really weird that week, too, in a way that's hard to describe; as if part of me was listening for sounds or voices just beyond my normal range. It made me feel very slightly deranged.

It's a good thing you're not going to be an agent, Melanie, I thought gloomily. When it comes to promoting Peace on Earth, a nutty angel is not your first choice of personnel.

Can you believe I still hadn't told my mates about my decision? They knew something was off, obviously. They're my mates. I think maybe they didn't like to hassle me.

That night Lola and I had arranged to hook up. I'd mentioned that Indigo had recommended FEATHERS, and she was keen to check it out. She turned up looking absolutely angelicious in a gauzy fairy dress with clumpy boots, that shouldn't go, but actually *totally* did!

Me? I was wrapped in a glamorous Angel Academy towel. Water dripped pathetically from my hair. "I'm late, aren't I?" I said guiltily.

Lola gave me the look we call her La Sanchez look. "This is getting to be a habit, Boo. Being late, leaving early, cancelling at the last minute."

"I'm really sorry, Lollie. I just got, you know, held up."

"Yeah, in your bathroom," she said in a sour voice.

I desperately tried to fake some party sparkle. "No, truly, I've been looking forward to this for *days*!"

"Oh, I *know*!" she said insincerely. "What's that B-thing you're always saying? 'The best buzz about being an angel, is boogying with buddies who just saved your booty'? Funny," she added. "I haven't heard you say that in a while."

She knows, I thought.

I took a shaky breath. "I really didn't mean to tell you like this, but I don't think I'm actually cut out to be that kind of angel."

I'd like to tell you my soul-mate was incredibly understanding. She wasn't. She was unbelievably hurt, and when Lola feels hurt she tries to hide it by blowing her top. We had a hugely distressing conversation, in which I never *once* managed to say how I really felt.

It was only after Lola stormed out, that I realised what I should have said. "I can't be your kind of angel, because I can't bear to see anyone get hurt EVER, like the PODS hurt you in Jamaica." Now it was too late.

This wasn't the first time we'd had a big fight. But that night it truly felt as if it was the last.

I was so upset, I did what they tell you in advice columns; lit a squillion scented candles, ran a hot bath, squirted in my fave rose bath essence, and climbed in for a good cry.

I'd deliberately put my stereo on continuous play. Unfortunately I'd left the Japanese harp CD in. I was up to my ears in bubbles by the time I realised, so I just let the atmospheric sounds wash over me. Actually it was kind of soothing, so when I went to bed, I left it on; and fell asleep with Japanese harps plinking in my ear.

When the phone rang I was so deeply asleep I couldn't find the handset for ages. "Melanie speaking," I mumbled. "Oh, hi, Michael! I thought you were away."

"I was," said the familiar deep voice. "Until an hour ago. Something came up and I had to come back."

I don't know your headmaster, obviously, but I'm fairly sure that Michael isn't like any headmaster you've ever come across on Earth.

That's probably because he's an archangel, one of the major powers behind the Agency. Michael also has special responsibilities for Earth, so he's constantly zooming off to historical hot spots. He sounded very tired, and also worried.

"I'll get straight to the point. We need two volunteers for an urgent soul-retrieval."

My inner angel sighed with relief. So that's what was going on!

"Jessica Lightpath suggested I approach you," Michael was saying. "She was impressed with your performance on her course."

If I'd been awake, I'd have launched into my sad story about giving up trouble-shooting. But Helix just jumped in with both feet.

"Have you asked Reuben?"

"Reuben's next on my list," said Michael.

"Then tell him I'm in."

Having kicked me out of my nice warm bed, Helix was making me hunt through my cupboards. I balanced the phone in the crook of my neck, while I hunted for the well-worn combats I thought I'd hung up for ever. "So whose soul are we meant to be retrieving?"

"Her name is Tsubomi." Michael pronounced it Sue-bo-mee.

"Sounds Japanese," I said, trying to climb into my combats without putting the phone down.

"Yes, she's from twenty-first century Japan."

"So what's the cosmic protocol? Do we go to Japan first, or buzz directly to Limbo or what?"

My inner angel was moving too fast even for Michael.

"Melanie, I think I should warn you that Tsubomi's situation is not as straightforward as the scenarios you practised on the course."

Helix and I finally succeeded in zipping up my trousers one-handed. "OK, you've warned me. So what is the situation exactly?"

There was a short silence on the other end, then Michael said, "This girl isn't actually dead."

There were four of us in the viewing suite. Me, Reuben, Michael and Sam, Michael's assistant. The lights were off, so I didn't see Reuben's expression when Tsubomi's face flashed up on the screen; I just heard him catch his breath.

Tsubomi was one of the most beautiful girls I have ever seen, but her face was totally empty. The mysterious inner light that made Tsubomi "Tsubomi", had gone.

A forest of wires and tubes connected her to the beeping gurgling machines that were keeping her body alive.

I swallowed hard. You see, I knew this girl.

I can't tell you where I knew Tsubomi from; like, if we'd both been temple dancers in a past life. I knew her, that's all. I could feel invisible cosmic strings running from her struggling heart to mine, and it really upset me. Because things didn't look good for Tsubomi; they didn't look good at all.

I was only thankful we weren't at her bedside for real. Seeing it on-screen was distressing enough. This young girl was literally on the brink of death, and two furious women were arguing across her bed. They were squabbling, if you can believe this, about who was to blame for Tsubomi taking an accidental overdose. Don't ask me how that was supposed to help.

The woman who looked as if she might be Tsubomi's mum, was practically spitting. "It's obvious you've never had children! You should have given the tablets to me. I'd have made sure she took the correct dose."

The other woman wore clingy leather that probably cost a bomb, but made her look disturbingly like Cat Woman. She was so angry you could hear her jewellery rattling. "The girl was exhausted, you stupid COW. We'd signed a million-dollar contract. She couldn't do the fashion shoot with freaking great shadows under her eyes."

"LOOK at her!" shrieked Tsubomi's mum. "Does my daughter look like she can do a fashion shoot to you! Three weeks she's been lying here like a zombie. THREE WEEKS."

A nurse rushed in. "Mrs Hoshi," she said reproachfully, "this kind of behaviour will not help your daughter's recovery."

"The only thing that can help her is a miracle!" Tsubomi's mum snapped.

"Miracles happen. I have witnessed several here in this room," the nurse insisted.

Mrs Hoshi looked contemptuous. "This is life, not TV. My daughter is not going to be 'touched by an angel'. She's probably going to be a vegetable for the rest of her days."

The nurse took a breath. "I'm sure the doctor told you that when someone is in a deep coma, their hearing is unusually acute. Please don't let your daughter hear you saying these negative things. Tell her you love her, that you want her to get better. Play her favourite songs."

"You just don't get it! This stupid girl had the world at her feet, but she was weak just like her father, and she just threw it all away!"

"Mrs Hoshi, you are speaking about your child!" The nurse made an effort to control her temper. "Why don't you go and get some coffee."

She slid a disk into the CD player on Tsubomi's bedside table. A sunny, boppy, totally forgettable pop song filled the room.

"Play something else," a voice pleaded.

For the first time I noticed the man slumped in the corner. His eyes were red from weeping, and he looked like he hadn't slept for weeks.

"That must be her dad," I murmured to Reuben. "So who's Cat Woman, do you reckon?"

"Miss Kinshō is Tsubomi's agent," Michael's assistant murmured.

I was gobsmacked. "Her *agent*! That's Tsubomi *singing*!"

"It's the first track she recorded. It topped the charts for weeks."

"She called it 'Bubble-gum Music'," Tsubomi's father was saying on-screen. "She told me once she wished every last copy could be melted down." He fumbled in his jacket and brought out a disk. "I brought this. I thought it might bring back happy memories."

"Of you?" jeered Mrs Hoshi. "You were never there! You were always shut away in your stupid workshop."

Tsubomi's father looked ashamed. "I run a small business, making traditional musical instruments," he explained humbly to the nurse. "When Mi-chan was small, she liked to hear me play the koto."

"She doesn't care about that! Do you always have to make such a fool of yourself?" Mrs Hoshi hissed at her husband.

He gave her a pained smile, "You were a fool once, Mariko, before you let this new love affair destroy our lives."

"Love affair!" She was outraged. "What are you babbling about?"

Mr Hoshi's voice was only just audible. "Your love affair with money."

"I'm not staying here to be insulted!" Mrs Hoshi stormed out and Miss Kinshō rushed after her. We could hear them yelling at each other in the corridor. The nurse shot out to calm things down.

Mr Hoshi looked down at the beautiful empty face of his daughter.

"Mi-chan, what have we done to you?" he asked in a broken voice. "I didn't mean to let so much distance grow between us. I was just so busy and your mother seemed to – well, she gave me the impression you were both managing fine without me. But I should have realised..." Tsubomi's dad was weeping openly. He took his daughter's limp hand and stroked it. "Come back, Mi-chan," he whispered. "Give me a second chance."

I was stealthily blowing my nose, so it took me longer than it should have done to register the music drifting from the speakers.

"Omigosh, I just bought this CD!" I gasped. "I was listening to it like, an hour ago!"

Reuben sounded choked up. "I don't get it. Why would a beautiful, talented, fourteen year old try to kill herself?"

Sam slid a disk into the DVD. "Technically speaking, this is classified cosmic material. But we thought you needed to see it."

He clicked a key and the hospital scene dissolved.

The Agency had been making a documentary of Tsubomi's life. They had film footage going back to when she was born. An MTV-type montage showed her growing up from a chubby baby, to a four-year-old tot in pyjamas, solemnly looking out at the night sky while her daddy sang and played some kind of Japanese harp, to a six-year-old cutie singing happily to herself, as she swung to and fro on a swing. Her mother watched from a doorway.

There's a look humans get when they get too close to the Dark Powers. You absolutely can't mistake it.

"They seemed like ideal parents for Tsubomi," Michael said. "Yakusho Hoshi was a skilled craftsman and musician, who inspired his daughter with a love of music. His wife, Mariko, was a former singer who quickly recognised her daughter's talent. Sadly, she saw Tsubomi's gift as a means to acquire money and power for herself."

On-screen, a stressed Mrs Hoshi was giving Tsubomi a singing lesson. "SMILE! SPARKLE!" she commanded. "Eyes and teeth, Mi-chan! Eyes and TEETH!"

In the next clip we saw a ten-year-old Tsubomi being pushed on to a makeshift stage to sing to a room full of unimpressed OAPs.

It was a dire song, and Tsubomi looked hugely uncomfortable. Yet even then you could see she was a star in the making.

When Tsubomi was twelve years old, her mother entered her for a well-known TV talent show. Mrs Hoshi was determined to make the all-male judges sit up and take notice. And, oh boy, did they take notice!

This sweet twelve year old bounded in front of the cameras, dressed in the kind of school uniform that would get any real schoolgirl expelled on the spot. With her blouse knotted above her navel, and literally flashing her knickers, Tsubomi belted out a cheesy pop number, doing things with her pelvis that would have shocked my nan to the core.

"Is Mrs Hoshi NUTS?" I hissed to Reuben. "She shouldn't be exploiting Tsubomi like this!"

"Shut your eyes and just listen," he hissed back.

This was sound advice. Without the disturbing visuals, Tsubomi's astonishing voice just shone through.

After her first album came out, Tsubomi totally dropped the bubble-gum sound, along with the jailbait clothes, and started writing her own material. Tsubomi's new songs were not only street, they had a genuine spiritual vibe, which fans instantly recognised. Since they were also wildly popular, neither her mum nor Miss Kinshō could exactly object.

While we were watching Tsubomi's life story, Michael made comments. "You see what she's doing? She's too young to be in the spotlight, yet she's trying to reach out to other young people. Tsubomi's only twelve here, yet she's already an artist through and through."

The assistant was more into family dynamics. Like, "Watch Mum's expression here. Did you see she's started wearing designer furs!" Or, "Have you noticed Dad is getting increasingly pushed out? You never see Dad on the concert tours. Just Mum and Miss Kinshō."

Tsubomi's schedule as a teenage celeb was unbelievably demanding. We saw her recording tracks for a new album, wisecracking on chat shows, doing interviews for lifestyle magazines, shooting videos, getting up at four a.m. to film a commercial for a mobile phone company.

Any time Miss Kinshō got caught on camera, she looked like the smug cat that got the low-fat cream. Just like a cat, she was completely two-faced. If it suited her, she'd schmooze around people and be really sweet and charming, but even a child could see she was out for herself. Tsubomi's mum didn't even bother with the charm.

One day Tsubomi took time out, to have some fun with her old school friends. They went shopping, took silly photos of themselves in these really cool Japanese photo booths, ate sushi. Then Tsubomi persuaded them to go with her to get a bad-girl tattoo!

When I saw the design on her naked shoulder, I almost stopped breathing. It was a tiny blue butterfly. The Universe had been sending me all these signs and I had never noticed.

Sam rapidly fast-forwarded through the next few scenes. "Miss Kinshō isn't too pleased as you can imagine," he commented. "Tsubomi never sees her friends after that. Mum takes care of that."

"Still with us, Melanie?" Michael inquired.

Still reeling from the butterfly coincidence, I forced myself to focus. My headmaster wanted me to see the second and final time Tsubomi dared to rebel.

It was the night they were due to play in Kyoto. Tsubomi had never been to this ancient city, and she badly wanted to do some sightseeing. Mariko Hoshi had a headache, and Miss Kinshō was prowling up and down, talking on her phone, so Tsubomi sneaked out of the hotel with one of her bodyguards.

Tsubomi and Stretch were good mates. We'd already seen them playing card games in the tour bus to pass the time. One time, when Mrs Hoshi was asleep, they had this mad competition to see how many takeaway noodles they could cram into their mouths!

Stretch never treated Tsubomi like a big star. He called her "Suzie", and said she reminded him of his little sister. I think he felt sorry for her, actually. OK, she was rich and famous, but she had absolutely no life.

Stretch agreed to help her play hooky, unwisely as it turned out.

Wearing dark glasses and with baseball caps pulled down over their faces, they wandered through old Kyoto. They ambled along canals fringed with weeping willows, visited a Zen garden made out of swirls of white gravel, and took photos at all the major tourist attractions. Then Tsubomi decided to hit the shops. She wanted to find a place she'd read about that sold a Japanese pickle her father adored.

This was a v. interesting cosmic coincidence, since one of our agents was conveniently playing his sax outside this exact same shop.

The Agency was increasingly alarmed by Mariko Hoshi's unhealthy influence on Tsubomi. They had big plans for this young girl, but if things didn't change, their budding star would be burned out before she was twenty.

So they called Blue in to help nudge Tsubomi's life back on track.

Blue is an Earth angel who is also a totally luminous sax player, and an old hand at giving cosmic reminders. When Tsubomi heard the divine sounds he coaxed from that sax, she responded exactly as our agents hoped. You could see her thinking, *Ohh, yesss! This is what it's all about. Not chat shows, not money, not fashion shoots. It's the music!*

She stood on that busy street corner for over an hour, totally rapt. Looking her in the eye, Blue started to play one of Tsubomi's own tunes, and being a true musician, she couldn't resist the invitation.

Outside the pickle shop, with traffic rushing past, the pop star and the undercover angel improvised a magical jam session.

Astonished passers-by couldn't believe these talented performers were playing for free. They literally started throwing paper money. Bank notes just snowed down. It was like one of those feel-good music videos. Little kids were dancing. Stretch was dancing. Old people with Zimmer frames were dancing. Reubs and I were dancing in the viewing suite!

But, inevitably, someone recognised her. A crowd quickly formed, fans began pushing and shoving, demanding autographs.

Stretch was excellent at his job. He managed to get Tsubomi away from the overexcited crowd and safely back to the hotel. Neither of them realised Tsubomi had been spotted by a photographer.

Next morning her picture was splashed all over the tabloids. Tsubomi Hoshi singing outside a pickle shop, with a homeless lowlife. Stretch was fired the same day.

Sam fast-forwarded to a few weeks later. Tsubomi was hunched in the back of a limo on the way to some TV studios. Since the pickle-shop incident she wasn't sleeping well. Looking unbelievably lost and lonely, she glanced out of the limo window, and totally froze.

Every billboard carried a giant poster of Tsubomi Hoshi!

My mates and I used to dream of being celebs. But when you lived the dream for real, like Tsubomi, it looked a lot more like a nightmare.

This marked the beginning of a worrying change in Tsubomi. On stage, she still sparkled to the max. But when the lights went down she looked absolutely drained.

"Omigosh! That's not tiredness," I said suddenly. "That's—"

Reuben shushed me. "We know what it is."

The documentary showed a few highlights from one of her last concerts, then replayed them from Tsubomi's point of view. Now we were looking out over a crowded concert hall. The huge space was packed out with ecstatic teenagers, swaying and singing along. All of them were waving cigarette lighters, making it look like the hall was full of twinkling fireflies. As the camera panned along the front row, there was a sudden technical glitch. Bizarre blips and blots of shadow made it impossible to see faces clearly. But I'd seen enough to know that the "fans" whose vibes were playing havoc with the Agency's equipment were not blissfully swaying, and they definitely weren't waving lighters. That's because PODS are allergic to light.

Sam touched a computer key, bringing up Tsubomi's energy field on the screen, a shimmery cloud of rose, gold and violet. "See those dark areas that look like bruises? Every concert, she gets a few more. The poor kid's on stage almost every night, there's no time for her to heal."

No wonder Tsubomi couldn't sleep. The miracle was she still had a vague memory of what she'd come to Earth to do. When PODS mess with your system, remembering who you are, and why you came to Earth, is generally the first thing to go.

I knew all this. What I didn't know was WHY? Why would the PODS go out of their way to target a teenage pop star? What threat could a sweet fourteen year old possibly pose?

Unless...

"You'd lined up some major cosmic role for Tsubomi, hadn't you?" I said suddenly. "And the Dark Agencies picked up on it?"

"That's very astute of you, Melanie," sighed Michael. "And as we've seen too often, Dark agents prefer to let humans do their dirty work for them."

I remembered the chilling expression in Mariko Hoshi's eyes, and shivered. "They'd got to work on her mum hadn't they?"

Sam put the film on pause. "And they brought Miss Kinshō in, and made sure Mr Hoshi was nudged out of the picture," he explained, "making it almost inevitable that Tsubomi would be pushed out into the spotlight years earlier than the Agency had intended."

"Then they sat back," said Michael, "and waited for her to sabotage herself."

I swallowed. It would never have occurred to those cosmic lowlifes that this vulnerable teenager would STILL try to carry out a soul plan designed for an older, wiser Tsubomi, like, *years* in the future.

Sam restarted the film. "There's not much more."

I wondered if the Dark Agencies had been filming Tsubomi too, playing the tapes in some viewing suite in the Hell dimensions, watching and waiting, hoping to find a way in. I think they were, because in the very next scene they got frighteningly close.

Tsubomi had flown to yet another city, to perform at a huge concert the next day. When they arrived there was some hassle with their luggage. The airline had lost the trunk with Tsubomi's stage costumes.

Mariko Hoshi stayed to sort it out. Tsubomi and her entourage went on to the hotel, only there'd been some major mix-up, her bodyguards and roadies hadn't been booked in and at two a.m. there were absolutely no vacancies. Which is how Tsubomi came to be sitting alone in an empty hotel lobby in the small hours, while a yawning Miss Kinshō signed the register.

Tsubomi was so exhausted she kept nodding off. The Agency cameras were playing up again. The ugly blips and blots made it impossible to identify the shadowy figures stealthily moving towards her across the foyer. Tsubomi's mineral water bottle slipped out of her hand and rolled across the floor. She jolted awake, and whoever or whatever she saw scared her so badly that her screams echoed round the foyer.

Miss Kinshō hurried towards her. "Tsubomi? What's wrong?"

The documentary cut to Mariko Hoshi and Miss Kinshō drinking saki at the Hoshi's apartment. They were celebrating their latest deal. A multinational wanted Tsubomi to promote a new teen clothing range. Tsubomi was all set to go global.

Mr Hoshi was sitting with them, but it was obvious he wasn't part of the celebration. He looked withdrawn and unhappy. The camera showed Tsubomi nervously hovering outside the door, wearing her fave Hello Kitty pyjamas. In that moment you saw how young she was, and how fragile. She took a breath, went in and made her big announcement.

"Mum, Dad, Miss Kinshō. I don't want to do this any more. I don't think I can. I want to make music because I love it, not because I have to, not because I'm scared of letting everyone down."

I have never ever heard a mother talk to her daughter the way Mariko Hoshi talked to Tsubomi then. It was a barrage of pure hate.

By the end Tsubomi was trembling, but you could see she still had one faint hope. She looked pleadingly at her father. "Dad?"

"I prefer to leave this type of decision to your mum," he mumbled.

Tsubomi closed her eyes. "Yes, Daddy, you do," she said in a choked voice. "And I wish you wouldn't."

Without another word she went to her room.

Weeks passed. Snowflakes melted in crowds on the window of the coach. Tsubomi and her entourage were on the road again.

Her insomnia was getting worse. Miss Kinshō had persuaded a doctor to prescribe super-strong sleeping tablets, as none of the normal ones seemed to work.

On nights she couldn't sleep, Tsubomi sat up watching Manga cartoons, or flicking through teen magazines, but mostly she played computer games. "I'll just get to the next level," she'd tell herself. "Then I'll stop." I knew she was really too scared to fall asleep.

One of our agents, posing as a roadie, tried to tell her that the pills were a bad idea.

"I have to sleep, don't I, Tomo?" she said softly. "I can't perform if I can't sleep." She suddenly looked confused. "How many pills did I just take then? Did you see? How many are left in the bottle?"

"You just took two," he said gently. "I was watching."

The following night, Tsubomi collapsed in a hotel bathroom.

By the time they found her, she'd slipped into a deep coma. We saw weeping fans leaving bouquets of flowers and flickering tea lights outside the Hoshi's apartment as if Tsubomi had already died.

The screen froze on the blank beautiful face in the hospital bed.

No one spoke.

It took me a few moments to pull myself together. "I don't mean to be dense, but do human souls often take off when their body falls into a coma?"

Michael seemed horrified. "Of course not. What kind of Universe do you think this is? Tsubomi has been under intolerable pressure. We believe she was protecting herself the only way she knows how."

"But she's in danger, isn't she? Not just from the Dark Agencies. The longer her soul is separated from her body, the more difficult it will be to retrieve."

Reuben cleared his throat. "Can I just ask a really obvious question? Tsubomi's been in a coma for three weeks. Why didn't some Agency guys go in straight away and get her back?"

"Erm, actually," admitted Sam, "she's sort of given us the slip."

I was gobsmacked. "You've lost a soul? I thought that was virtually impossible!"

"It is. But Tsubomi is an unusual girl. And remember we're talking about a million plus Limbo dimensions. We simply don't have enough personnel to search them all."

It was down to me to ask the second most obvious question.

"So this wasn't like, Tsubomi's time to die?"

"No," Michael said. "It isn't Tsubomi's time to die."

"But she still could?"

"Yes, she still could," he said very quietly.

"If you don't know where she is, how exactly are we supposed to bring her back?" asked Reuben.

Michael took a breath. "There is one technique which might enable us to find her, but there would have to be a soul connection between the human and at least one of the agents."

I shot up in my seat. "But there IS a link! I've been feeling it for days. I just didn't realise until tonight."

"We suspected there might be." Michael sounded relieved.

"It's theoretically possible to locate a lost soul by using the principle of resonance," Sam explained.

"Like sound, you mean?" I said.

"More like vibration. It's an ancient and extremely powerful angelic technique. I'd say it works nine times out of ten. The only drawback is, we wouldn't be able to track you. There'd be no Agency backup."

Reuben grinned. "No change there then!"

"How *will* we cope!" I sighed.

"Sam, have you noticed trainees today have no respect?" Michael complained.

"Actually, I seem to remember you making the same comments about me," Sam said tactfully. "So are you guys willing to give it a shot?"

"Yeah, we're in, aren't we, Mel?" said Reuben immediately.

"I'd like to hear it from Melanie, if you don't mind," Michael gave me one of his searching looks. "I heard you were thinking of changing options?"

Once again my inner angel got in first. "That's OK," she said, quickly. "Might as well go out with a bang."

It seemed like Helix REALLY wanted to go on this mission.

"Nobody wants to pressure you," Sam said cautiously. "But pretty much everyone here feels you and Reuben are exactly the right people to help Tsubomi. You're young, you both have a great love of music, and I think you're on very similar wavelengths."

Reuben sounded distressed. "It's not just about Tsubomi, is it? In Heaven, everything reminds kids how magic they are. On Earth there's all this constant pressure to forget. Tsubomi used her songs to help teenagers remember who they really are. Those kids need her, and they need her songs."

At that moment it hit me just why Tsubomi Hoshi was so dangerous.

The Dark Powers want humans to live in a kind of

grey-green-khaki waking dream. Tired, depressed, confused. Awake enough to work, shovel in food and watch TV. Asleep enough to make them easy to control.

This extraordinary fourteen year old had the power to wake kids up all over the world.

We said goodbye to Michael out in the corridor. He'd been called away from some huge Earth project to deal with Tsubomi; now he had to go back. "Sam will talk you through the procedure. It's really very simple." Michael sounded slightly anxious.

I could see he felt he was abandoning us. To make him feel better I teased, "If we complete this mission, Michael, you have to take us to Guru for hot chocolate!"

He gave me a tired smile. "If you complete this mission, I'll take you to Sugar Shock. I've heard their hot chocolate is out of this world."

Then we tried not to notice we'd both said "if".

Sam led us along a maze of corridors to a row of lifts I'd never used before. I couldn't tell you if we travelled up or down to reach the Zone, as Sam kept calling it. When the lift doors slid open we were in a totally unfamiliar part of the Agency Tower. A sign said:

TRANSDIMENSIONAL TRAVEL ZONE
PERMIT HOLDERS ONLY BEYOND THIS POINT

Our previous missions started in a bustling departure lounge. It's mad up there, no matter what time you go: trainees dressed in costumes from every historical period you can think of, all queuing for angel tags, making last minute calls, joking with team mates, attempting to meditate while the maintenance staff send for some crucial replacement part for their time portal.

In comparison, the Zone was as silent as the bottom of the ocean.

Sam unlocked a series of sealed doors made from some special celestial metal, ushered us through the final door and relocked it.

When I saw the flotation tanks, I understood why they were kept sealed off from the rest of Angel HQ. Those things were SCARY. "Tank" generally makes you think of water, but these containers held a particularly high-octane cosmic energy. The minute I walked in, I felt my hair fizz with electricity.

Miniature bolts of lightning were literally crackling around Reuben's dreads.

"OK, Beeby?" he inquired calmly.

"I'm fine," I squeaked.

The energy in the tanks didn't stay still for a second. It bubbled and swirled, constantly changing colour.

"You said you wanted to go out with a bang," Reubs commented.

I realised this was the first he'd heard of my change of plan.

"I was going to tell you, honestly—"

"Hey, I didn't take it personally. My name's not Brice! And it's not Orlando, either," he added in a meaningful tone.

He was talking about the angel boy who'd broken my heart.

"You're such a fab friend," I told him emotionally. "You know what's so great? There's never any silly complications with you. You're like, the *ultimate* star brother!"

For a second there was this funny little vibe. Then Reuben's smile was back in place.

"Just my luck to be everyone's fave big brother!" he grinned.

Sam coughed. He was waiting to run through the procedure for this type of transdimensional travel. And then we had to do it for real.

Did I explain we had to totally *immerse* ourselves in this energy? I'm not exaggerating; it feels almost exactly like you're drowning in light. Though when you're drowning, you probably don't feel your molecules melting back into their pure energy form.

I reminded myself sternly that this was an ancient angelic procedure. The concept of Extreme Angelic Melting was not exactly appealing, but if they'd been using it for aeons, it had to be safe, right?

And anyway, Reuben was in the tank next to mine, and there was absolutely no reason why I should have another cosmic freak-out. To give myself extra courage, I started to sing our anthem. "We're not alone," I sang squeakily. "We're not alone."

Sadly, I'm such a wuss that I'm capable of singing uplifting anthems AND thinking scary thoughts simultaneously!

The lights above the tanks dimmed.

Not the best moment to remember Sam's throwaway comment that this ancient angelic technique worked "nine times out of ten".

OMIGOSH! I panicked. Suppose this is the tenth one today?

Too late to back out now. Numbers were flashing in the corner of the tank, some scary unstoppable countdown.

TEN, NINE, EIGHT...

And then I saw her. I saw Tsubomi floating in front of me, like a ghost, if ghosts wore Hello Kitty T-shirts, baseball caps and jeans.

"Tsu—Tsubomi?" I whispered. My voice sent gold and silver shock waves rippling through the tank.

Her lips parted, and I suddenly knew she was calling my name.

She wants *us to come and find her*, I thought.

...**SEVEN, SIX**...

Soul connections are a truly wonderful thing. Now Tsubomi had made contact I wasn't afraid. I didn't even mind that my molecules were dissolving into pure energy. I was free! Free to fly in any direction. Take me to her, wherever she is, I willed, take me to Tsubomi Hoshi now.

...**FIVE, FOUR, THREE**...

Something was happening, a peculiar sensation like a kite slipping free of its string.

...**TWO, ONE, ZERO!**

The simmering shimmering colours vanished.

Like a bird released from a cage, my soul went soaring off to a totally unknown dimension.

CHAPTER FOUR

Light flickered high above me.

I could hear crickets chirping and the buzz of summer bees. The air was so humid it was literally steaming. I was lying on warm damp earth, looking up into the branches of a tree. Sparkling drops slid off the leaves, and splashed on to my skin. We'd obviously just missed a heavy downpour.

"Phew! We actually made it to... wherever this is!"

I felt Reuben's voice reverberating through my skull bones. We were lying head to head like little kids.

Bones? I thought in surprise. Heads? Didn't we just dissolve?

We sat up and stared at each other in dismay.

"Oh, well," Reubs sighed. "Mustn't be picky."

"It's all right for you, you don't care what you look like!"

"What are you complaining about, girl? That straw hat is totally you!" He patted my bare foot. "Pity they couldn't stretch the budget to include footwear!"

Neither of us had the slightest idea why we were dressed like poor Japanese peasants, but then absolutely nothing was what we expected.

The Limbo dimensions we'd experienced in simulations were creepy colourless places, almost like you were trapped inside CCTV. This world was GORGEOUS! I felt as if I'd fallen into an old Japanese painting, one of those old scrolls, with a *très* deep poem written in exquisite Japanese calligraphy.

This would have to be a summer poem, I decided dreamily. It would describe the way the sunlight made patterns on the forest floor, and the blissful warmth on our skin. Ohh, and the mind-melting scent of flowers after the rain...

I should just mention, that despite its beauty, this world had the most peculiar vibe. Reubs and I agreed it was unlike anything we'd ever come across before. It wasn't necessarily an ominous-type vibe, but it kind of made you wonder if there might be more to this place than met the eye.

At the same moment, we noticed the bag hanging in a tree.

"Oh, that's for us," I said confidently.

Reuben looked bewildered. "How do you know that?"

I shook my head. "I just know."

"Wowie!" he said sarcastically, as he unhooked the crude leather satchel. "The perfect accessory for our scuzzy outfits!"

"Now now!!" I teased. "Thought we weren't going to be picky!"

The bag turned out to contain another bag. It was actually more like a miniature sack, filled to the brim with what looked like peach stones.

"Oh-kay," said Reuben. "I'm sure it's very nice of the local spirits to give us their old peach stones."

"Actual peaches would have been much nicer," I agreed, peering annoyingly over his shoulder. "But then there'd be that age-old Limbo dilemma of ooh, should we risk eating them or not! What's that other thing? The rolled up paper?"

"You girls are sooo impatient!" Reuben made a big deal of extracting the scroll from the bag, slowly untying the grubby piece of cord and unrolling the parchment inch by inch, until I threatened to thump him.

"Sweetpea if you don't let me see it NOW, you're going to be SO sorry," I told him, getting genuinely peeved, as he held it tantalisingly out of reach. Then I saw his stunned expression.

"D minus for refreshments, spirits," he murmured. "But a definite A plus for map drawing!"

I've had some bizarre experiences since I've been in the angel biz, but this was the first time either of us had come across actual magic. And the spirit map was magic, without a shadow of a doubt. The vibrant technicoloured markings were busily rearranging themselves even as we watched. First they showed a close-up of our immediate surroundings, then we got a kind of aerial view of how it all fitted together.

"Oh, *man*," said Reuben in a weird voice.

When I saw the tiny blue butterfly pulsing in the corner of the map, my heart actually stumbled over a beat. The mysterious map maker was showing us where to find Tsubomi!

Jessica had mentioned the possibility of running into helpful spirits in Limbo, but I didn't remember her mentioning them drawing maps.

All my misgivings totally faded away. This was going to be a doddle! We'd survived Extreme Angelic Melting and we'd located exactly the right dimension by using our own natural magnetism. Now we had a helpful flashing butterfly to show us which way to go. Missions don't get much more jammy than this, I thought happily.

Following the path indicated on the map, we made our way out of the trees into a sparkling rain-washed world.

Reuben was enchanted. "This is like a dream."

"So pure angels do dream, then?"

This was something I was always meaning to ask.

"It's a phrase, Beeby!"

"Sorry! I forgot you guys don't actually need to sleep!"

Reuben was looking down at the ground with a perplexed expression. "This ought to kill our feet," he said. "There's stones and all sorts in this mud."

"Maybe Limbo feet are tougher?" I suggested.

I felt heaps tougher in general. It was getting really hot and the air was loads more humid than I'm used to, yet I was twinkling over the ground like Tinkerbell.

Girls were planting seedlings in flooded fields beside the road. They waded knee-deep in the muddy water, singing as they worked, a truly heart-rending melody. Reuben reckoned they were singing in medieval Japanese. This could be true, but I couldn't seem to get past their strong country accents.

"They're asking the god of rice to come down and bless their seedlings, so they'll get a good harvest," he explained.

"Think we can spare a few minutes to send vibes?" I asked.

Discreetly as possible, we beamed uplifting vibes at the waterlogged fields. I didn't think the girls had noticed us, but as we walked away, a few waved rather wearily, and one called something that sounded like, "Hope you find her!"

"Was there something weird about that?" asked Reuben, after we'd gone past.

"Yeah, like, how did *she* know?"

He shook his head. "Not that. Didn't you get the

feeling if you were to come by tomorrow, those girls would be doing exactly the same thing?"

"I see what you mean," I said slowly. "Like they were just there for local colour or whatever. Do you think they stopped singing once we were out of sight?"

"Or stopped *existing*," he suggested.

I shivered. "That's not funny."

Jessica had constantly warned us: "Limbo is a world of traps and tricks. Never trust anything or anyone."

"When I think about it," I admitted, "they didn't seem exactly real. Not *real* real."

"And the birds are wrong," he said suddenly. "They sound right, but they fly all wrong."

I burst out laughing. "What's that supposed to mean? Like, they're going backwards!"

"Don't snigger, Beeby," he said sternly. "Just look and learn."

My buddy spun me round, and pointed me at a patch of sky. After a few seconds a line of wild geese, or it could have been swans, flew out of some trees and disappeared towards a line of hills, making their sad honking cry.

"And this is interesting because?"

"Keep watching and you'll find out."

Reuben was counting under his breath. He got as far as twenty.

"Bingo!" he said triumphantly.

An identical line of long-necked birds flew out of the same cluster of trees and disappeared towards the same line of hills, with the same eerie cries.

"And they always fly right to left, never left to right," he said.

"So? They're probably migrating," I suggested vaguely.

"In *sevens*? I don't think so! There's always *exactly* seven birds. Not five or six or eight. Seven, exactly. Every time."

I didn't share Reuben's fascination with local bird behaviour, but he's my mate, after all, so we hung around for a bit to test his theory. And actually it was quite spooky. Every twenty seconds on the dot, exactly seven birds flew out of the trees and vanished at exactly the same point between the hills.

"They're like robot geese," he said in a baffled voice. "Same number of wing beats, same number of cries. I don't get it."

"Me neither," I sighed. "But we'd better get going."

A wicker carriage rattled past, drawn by two sweating horses. A lady was peeping shyly out of the window, half hiding her face with her fan.

Reubs and I were genuinely charmed by the sights we saw on the road. Then we discovered that all these charming scenes and characters invariably popped up again further down the road, which rather took the shine off. After a few hours, we were like, oh right, another shrine, and yet more atmospheric temple bells. Oh, and another coy lady riding by in a quaint wicker carriage. And yet another travelling musician carrying some sort of Japanese stringed instrument on his back. Super.

We continually consulted the map to see if we were any closer to Tsubomi. But the blue butterfly seemed as far away as ever.

Reuben had been unusually quiet. I just assumed he was still puzzling over the Riddle of the Birds, then he suddenly blurted out, "So is this like some old-time version of Japan or what?"

"It's definitely old-time Japanese-*ish*," I agreed.

We trudged along in silence for a few minutes.

"If you had to sum up the feeling in this world, in one word," my buddy asked in an earnest voice. "What would it be?"

"Reuben, it's a *world*. Worlds are full of zillions of different feelings."

He shook his head. "Think about the people we saw earlier. Singing peasant girls, carriage ladies, harp players. Seriously, what vibe did you get?"

"You mean, like 'beautiful but basically weird'?"

"Beautiful and weird, for sure. But don't you keep getting flashes of something *underneath* beautiful and weird?"

I frowned. "I'm not sure. Probably I'm not as sensitive as you, Sweetpea."

We were passing a shrine to some local god. It was the spitting image of all the other shrines we'd passed, but for the first time I found myself taking a closer look.

People had left offerings to the god; flowers and bowls of rice. A few had left toys and baby clothes. Local people had written prayers on scraps of paper, and tied them to tree branches. They fluttered in the breeze like tiny flags. I don't know what it was, but something about that little prayer tree suddenly made me want to cry.

I thought about the beautiful carriage ladies, with their pale mask-like make-up. I remembered how each one had turned at the last minute, to gaze pleadingly over her fan.

And that last harp player, sitting down in the middle of nowhere, plucking those haunting chords...

"Sad," I realised. "This place feels humongously sad."

Reuben nodded. "Have you ever been anywhere before where there's just one overwhelming vibe?"

I shook my head. "Never."

"Me neither."

After that last musician, we didn't see a soul for over an hour. So it was quite a shock when we passed the hermit sitting by his fire.

The old man had been living out in the wilds so long, he'd become a bit wild and woolly himself. His robes were dirty and torn, and his hair had practically grown down to his waist. He patiently fed pieces of broken bamboo into the flames, to keep the fire going under an old cooking pot. He peered out through his straggly hair, calling a friendly greeting. Remembering Jessica's warnings, we weren't sure if we should talk to him.

"It'd be good if he could tell us where we are," I whispered.

The spirit map was fabulous on rivers and mountains and aerial views but it didn't seem nearly so fussed about fiddly details like names!

"He's probably OK," Reuben decided.

So we said hi, and then we all did a lot of polite Japanese bowing.

The hermit invited us to drink tea with him but Jessica had warned us of the dangers of accepting food or drink.

"Oh, that's OK," I said awkwardly. "We honestly wouldn't want to put you to so much trouble."

"I can see you're not from this world!" The hermit's smile seemed surprisingly young in such a wrinkled old face.

I'd been hoping we just blended in, but obviously our peasant gear hadn't fooled him one bit.

He broke off a new piece of bamboo from a plant growing beside the road, bent over his pot and began whisking its contents to a froth. "I know who you seek," he said calmly. "And I know the trials that lie in wait, if you refuse to turn back."

I gulped. Did EVERYONE in this world know what we were up to? Did we have, like, a big sign: "*Soul-retrieval in Progress*"?

"Thanks," Reuben said gruffly. "But turning back is not an option."

The hermit carefully poured scalding green liquid into an earthenware cup. It looked suspiciously herbal to me. I wondered if this old man was some kind of Limbo wizard. Maybe we'd just interrupted him before he flung in eyes of newts and dead man's toenails?

He gave me an amused look. "This is a strange world to you, child. A strange, baffling, perilous world."

I felt myself going red. The old hermit had virtually read my thoughts!

"You are strangers here," he said gravely. "Without a guide, it is unlikely you will ever reach your destination, and no local will venture where you need to go. I advise you to leave while you still can!"

"We've got a job to do," said Reuben stubbornly. "Perils or no perils, guide or no guide, we're not leaving till it's done."

"You're already too late!" the hermit said to my dismay. "The dark lord already has your friend in his power."

"There's a dark lord! Are you sure?" I gasped. "How – what did he do?"

"Do such trivial details matter, child? He used his power! Didn't your teacher tell you the Dark Forces are more powerful in dimensions such as these?"

"Yes, she did, actually," I said defensively.

"And did she tell you they have almost driven out the ancient gods who once dwelled here?"

"No," I admitted. "But it was just a weekend course. Look, I'm really sorry about the nice gods baling out of your world, but we just have to save Tsubomi." I was close to tears. "We *have* to."

He frowned. "Why do you care about her so much? She is no kin to you."

"So? Rellies aren't always all that," I told him. "But you can meet a total stranger and you just know they're your family. Like, if Reuben ever needed me, I'd just drop everything and go."

"Ditto, Beeby," Reuben murmured.

The hermit's voice softened. "And that's how you feel about this girl?"

"She needed us," I said huskily. "So we came."

The old man shook his head. "If you want to save this girl's soul, you must walk the Demon Road."

It's just a name, I told myself quickly. It's not used by real demons.

"The road will lead you to the Palace of Endless Night. That is where the girl you seek is held captive. I would take you myself, but unfortunately I have business elsewhere. My blessings on your mission."

"But how do we—"

He'd gone. No shimmer, no puff of smoke. Just gone.

"…find the Demon Road?" I asked the empty space.

I almost stamped. "Can you believe that! He was a wizard after all! This world is just TOO *scary*."

"I don't think he was your average hermit," Reuben agreed.

"Jessica told us PODS can cloak their vibes in Limbo, but I totally forgot. He could have been a dark agent deliberately leading us away from Tsubomi."

Reuben shook his head. "He gave us his blessing. No PODS would do that."

I folded my arms. "OK, so if he wasn't PODS and he wasn't a wizard, what was he brewing in that manky pot?"

Reuben investigated the pan still steaming beside the fire.

"Smells like some kind of tea," he grinned.

We unrolled the map so we could check our progress.

Reuben blinked. "Now where did that come from?"

A glimmery green line had appeared to the left of the first track. The butterfly pulsed meaningfully over the new road.

"I don't get it. How come it didn't show up till now?"

"I have no idea," Reuben admitted. "But as you see, the butterfly has spoken. A more useful question might be, are we up for this?"

"Totally!" I said brightly. I want to go back to school and tell everyone we walked the Demon Road all the way to the Palace of Endless Night!"

"Psst," I added in a whisper. "That was my angel talking before. My legs are pure jelly, how about yours?"

"Pure and utter jelly!" he agreed.

"We'll do it on three!" I told him. "One, two, THREE."

We both made a wild synchronised leap to the left.

We'd been walking through a summer world of birds and flowers and sweet-earth smells; old-time Japan at its sunny best.

The instant we set foot on the Demon Road, this changed.

It was the same landscape, yet now it felt hideously ominous. Even the air was hideous – heavy and clammy, making it hard to breathe. And the chirping of summer insects that I barely noticed previously, now sounded like a v. v. disturbing track on one of Brice's Astral Garbage CDs.

You know on a sunny day, when a cloud unexpectedly covers the sun, how all the world's colours suddenly look deeply wrong? It was like that. Even the shrines felt wrong, with icky dark stains splattered on nearby tree roots and surrounding stones.

I could feel myself getting more and more twitchy. When absolutely everything feels creepy, it's hard to know if something's normal creepy, or, you know, *creepy*. All at once everything, even the Astral Garbage insects, went silent. At the same moment I realised the sun was starting to set.

Was I tempted to turn back? Duh! Was I ever!! But we had come to save Tsubomi, so we just kept going.

In the fading light, the Demon Road had acquired a faint green glimmer that made me think of poisonous slime. Maybe it was psychological, but

I was suddenly aware of an icky gluey sensation under my bare tootsies.

We'd been climbing steadily for over an hour. It was inevitable we'd have to go down at some point. Suddenly the slime trail veered off sharply downhill through a most unpleasant-looking grove of trees.

"I guess it's onwards and downwards to the Palace of Unending Night then?" I said bravely.

"I think you'll find that's actually the Palace of *Endless* Night, Melanie," Reubs corrected, taking off a girl from our class.

"Imagine having to deliver parcels to *that* address!" I giggled. "Care of The Dark Lord, Palace of Endless Night, beside the Demon Road."

"Imagine the kind of parcels!" he said darkly.

Cracking nervy jokes to hide our panic, we took the sinister left-hand fork.

Angels have a good relationship with trees as a rule. We like their vibes, they like ours. Not these trees, however. These trees had absolutely gone over to the dark side. I'm serious. I *twice* tripped over roots that I swear weren't there a second before, and don't even get me started on the sound FX. Whispering, mutterings, gibberings, moans. It didn't matter how fast you spun round, you could never see who was doing it.

"I suppose it makes sense," said Reuben. "Cosmic balance and all that. We've had the helpful spirits, now we're meeting up with the unhelpful ones."

"Could we talk about spirits when there's a bit more light, please?" My voice came out abnormally high.

"Do you think demons secrete something from their glands that makes the road glow like this, or is it an energy thing?" Reuben mused.

"Could we not say the D-word, either, please!" I squeaked.

The hill was sloping so steeply, I was getting vertigo just looking down. By the time we emerged back into what was left of the daylight, it was impossible to trudge at our normal pace. Soon we were hurtling downhill, skidding and scattering stones in a mad rush.

Minutes before we reached the bottom of the mountain, Reuben said, "Oh, *what*!"

We slithered to a standstill in a shower of gravel.

Below us was an old riverbed that must have dried up years ago. The ground was littered with rubble that had been washed here in the days when there was still a fast-flowing river.

If I squinted against the evening light, I could just make out a sheen, like a layer of evil lime jelly, glistening on the bottom of the riverbed. Marching across pebbles, and possibly old skulls and bits of human elbow, the Demon Road disappeared into the mouth of a humongous underground cavern.

"I didn't realise that other bit was the scenic part," Reuben said gloomily.

"Guess he must be a *really* dark lord," I said, attempting a joke.

A grazing animal moved down in the riverbed, catching my eye.

I watched it vaguely. There seemed to be quite a few down there. Suddenly I realised what I was seeing.

"Omigosh, Reuben! Those aren't animals, they're children!"

The sun was so low in the sky, we were half blinded by this time, so it took us a while to figure out what the little kids were doing.

"Some of those rocks are bigger than they are," Reuben muttered. "What kind of game involves lugging big boulders?"

"It's way too late for them to be out. Someone should tell them to go home before it gets dark."

We slithered the rest of the way down the mountain.

Close-up, the scene was even more surreal. Hordes of little children, some hardly more than babies, were frantically building a tower on the riverbank. They rushed about, feverishly collecting stones and piling them on their unstable construction. From their constant scared glances at the cavern, it seemed likely that the thing they were frightened of lived in there.

"Hi," Reuben said in a sympathetic voice. "You're working very hard."

They went on piling on boulders as if he hadn't spoken.

In my world, different sized rocks would make different kinds of sounds when you set them down. Here, every single stone landed with the same identical *clack*.

"It's probably time to go home now," I hinted. "It's getting dark and you must be getting hungry."

Some of the little ones started whispering among themselves. With their matted hair and mud-coloured clothes, they looked like they'd been formed out of the dried mud of the riverbed.

There was something seriously off about these kids. Their skin was crusted with dirt from the riverbed, so it was hard to tell for sure, but it totally didn't seem like a healthy colour.

"Is it the light, or do they look sort of *blue*?" I murmured to Reubs.

"Pick up the pace, you lot!" yelled one of the big boys. "We've got to finish this before it gets dark."

One little girl burst into tears. "You always say that, but we never do!"

The boy can't have been more than ten, but he tried to control his panic, and bent down to comfort the little tot. "It'll be different this time!" he promised. "You've all worked really well today. This is the best tower we've ever built. The gods have *got* to be pleased with this one."

The small girl wiped her nose on her mud-coloured sleeve. "And will they let us through the gate this time?"

He darted an anguished glance at the cave. "Yes, if you work fast."

"Will we see gates crusted with precious pearls?" she persisted.

"Yes, and the gates will swing open and they'll let us into the Pure Land, and we'll live happily ever after. Now MOVE!"

"The Pure Land," Reuben whispered. "Isn't that one of the names for Heaven?"

I felt the tiny hairs stand up on my arms. "Omigosh, Reubs! These kids are—"

I broke off. A small boy was creeping closer, clutching two enormous stones against his chest. He stared up at me with an awed expression.

"You're so pretty," he said reverently. "You must be from the Pure Land, like Jizo." He was exactly like a normal child, except for his haunted eyes and the cold blue skin showing through the dirt like mouldy lemon rind.

He stretched out a hand. I jerked away with a squeak. I was SO ashamed. I don't know why I was so freaked. Limbo is full of dead people. It's virtually a dead people convention.

Reuben is great in situations like these. He crouched down beside the little boy. "Want to put those down for a minute?" he suggested.

The little boy let his stones slip to the ground without a word, then he just leaned very wearily against Reubs, and put his thumb in his mouth.

Reuben patted his shoulder. "Are you sure the big boys have got their facts straight? You've really got to build a tall tower before you can get into the Pure Land?"

"Yes, it's a law." The little kid had to take his thumb out to talk.

"I don't think that can be right," Reuben said gently. "Heaven is for everyone. All souls go home to Heaven just as soon as they've finished with their bodies."

The boy shook his head. "We're not allowed. Because it's all our fault."

"What is?" Reuben looked totally bewildered.

"When you die young, it causes trouble for everyone," the child looked deeply ashamed. "That's why we have to be punished."

"For being *dead*?" I said in horror. "In what sick world does that make sense?"

He tried to smile. "It's OK. Soon we'll build a really good tower, and the gods will forgive us and open the gates into the Pure Land."

He glanced over at the children, madly piling on stones. *Clack. Clack. Clack.* To anyone over ten, it was heartbreakingly obvious what was going to happen. Poor mites, I thought, living out here in this horrible place, building towers that are totally doomed to fall down.

I crouched beside him. (Even I can't be scared of a dead kid who still sucks his thumb.) "Maybe we could help," I suggested.

I heard him suck in his breath. "No! That's cheating. We have to do it on our own. If we cheat he'll know." He darted another terrified glance towards the cavern. "It's getting dark. He'll be here any minute."

I had a sudden unpleasant suspicion.

"Are you sure these are gods, sweetheart? Are you sure they're not, erm, *demons*?"

The little boy clapped his hands over his ears. "Why did you say that?" he screamed. "You're not supposed to SAY that!"

The ground began to tremble. The children scattered, screaming in terror. A gust of foul-smelling wind surged out of the cavern. The wind swirled up to the tower, toppling it to the ground with a mighty roar. A hideous figure lumbered out of the cavern, brandishing a blazing torch, and howling with rage.

CHAPTER FIVE

Here's a little Limbo-type quiz for you.

A drooling three-eyed demon is staggering towards you, saying something deeply uncomplimentary in demon language. Do you:

   a) Take to the hills screaming like a girl?

   b) Shin up the nearest tree and hope he'll be gone by morning?

   c) Screw your eyes up tight and pray to wake up?

Erm, not if your name's Mel Beeby!

For no reason, I fell on my knees among the pebbles, and started grovelling in the bag, frantically trying to locate the peach stones. What's even weirder, is Reuben seemed to know what I was up to! At the same moment we yelled, "Catch!" and lobbed some of our peach-stone stash to the older kids, who also seemed to know exactly what was going on. We all began hurling peach stones at the demon.

Zoom, zoom, zoom! They didn't sound like normal peach stones, as they zipped through the air, but then they didn't behave like them either.

Did you know peach stones have a magical property that makes them ideal for fending off minor Japanese demons?

If someone bombarded you or me with fruit pits, we'd just get peppered with teeny bruises. When a peach stone comes into contact with a demon, it's a bit more dramatic. More like sprinkling salt on a huge slug.

Picture a demon-sized slug, staggering around the riverbed, howling in agony, as flying peach stones (*zoom, zoom, zoom*) made peach-stone sized holes in various unspeakable parts of its anatomy. Then picture all the demon's insides spurting out of the holes (euw!) and the demon toppling in agonising slow motion like a tree, and finally landing with a resounding thud (WHUMP!).

A stunned silence followed. Then all the kids went bananas, cheering, hugging each other and jumping up and down.

"Ding, dong, the evil demon is dead," I whispered. The kids seemed to be taking it in their stride, but I was completely traumatised. "How did we *know*?" I hissed to Reuben. "How did we know what to do?"

My buddy stared down at the dead demon with interest, as it slowly dissolved into icky demon jam. "How did you know to take the bag?" he inquired, sounding surprisingly matter-of-fact.

"True." I felt a flicker of interest. "Wonder what else I know in Limbo!"

Before he could answer, the children grabbed our hands and dragged us into their mad dance of celebration.

We were meant to be tracking Tsubomi through Limbo, but Reubs and I agreed it would be v. insensitive of us to just breeze off, like, "Byee!" So we chilled with the dead kids for a while. We lit a fire in the riverbed, and Reubs gave them some tips on tower building, and when no one was looking we beamed uplifting vibes. After a while the kids started looking uneasy.

"I don't mean to be rude, but isn't it time for you to go?" asked the oldest boy.

A girl rolled her eyes at him. "They're worried, stupid," she explained. "They don't like to think of us being out here on our own."

He looked surprised. "We're not alone. Jizo looks after us, when he can."

The little boy had mentioned someone called Jizo.

"He doesn't have three eyes does he?" I asked doubtfully.

"He's the god of all dead children," one of the older girls explained. "He should be living in the Pure Land, but he won't go until we're all safely inside."

Reuben looked touched. "Sounds like a cool god. Say hi to him, from us."

The oldest boy jumped up. "Take the demon's torch. It's still burning."

He tried to lift it but it was too heavy. Reuben stopped him, breaking it in two, in one smooth swift movement. Woo, I thought, but my buddy didn't seem to think he'd done anything unusual. He calmly lit a second torch from the first, and handed it to me.

The boy gave us a sheepish grin. "I forgot! We're supposed to give you this."

He reached inside his tattered shirt and handed me a strange little dagger. I thought daggers had to be made of metal, but this one was carved out of some jet-black stone. Tiny Japanese characters were written on it in gold.

"Its name is Heart Seeker," the boy told us solemnly. "You stick it in the dark lord's heart," he explained helpfully, in case the name wasn't enough of a clue.

The dagger gave off THE most disturbing vibe, so I quickly passed it to Reuben. He tested the blade with the edge of his finger.

"Thanks for this," he told the boy. "And good luck with that tower tomorrow. Remember, you want the flat stones at the bottom. Keep the bumpy ones for the top."

Walking carefully around the pool of demon jelly, we crossed the riverbed, holding our torches high.

We looked back at the children all waving and calling goodbyes.

"Ready?" said Reuben.

Turning our back on the firelight, we walked into the darkness.

*　*　*

According to the map, the road would lead us to the innermost core of the mountain. In practice, this seemed to involve going down and around, down and around, very much like descending a spiral staircase, except there were no actual stairs.

Underground, the road's evil shimmer had become a totally toxic glow. Our torches showed flickery glimpses of an eerie subterranean world; sudden scary cracks in the earth that emitted spurts of stinky steam and the dark glitter of bottomless underground pools.

Normally I'd be doing this running commentary, like, "Ooh, did you see that HUGE root that looked just like one of the seven dwarfs!" But I was too preoccupied. My thoughts had taken a most worrying turn.

"You've gone very quiet," Reuben commented after a while.

"I'm not that good underground," I admitted. "Plus…"

"What?"

I swallowed. "Something about all this just seems weirdly familiar."

"You think you've been here before?"

"I *know* I haven't been here before. YOU haven't been here before. Yet we both know all this – *stuff*. Stuff we have no business knowing."

"Like the bag?"

"Exactly. Then there's those birds that only fly in like, relays, exactly twenty seconds apart. Not to mention that bizarre peach stone episode. Then AFTER we kill the demon, and only then, a kid suddenly remembers he's supposed to give us a deeply suspect dagger, and what I don't understand is, *why* wasn't I more surprised?"

"Maybe you're remembering a simulation in Dark Studies?"

I shook my head. "It's not a heavenly memory. This is connected with Earth, I'm positive."

The underground road led us though a series of high-ceilinged caves. Finally, we came to this really massive cavern, like a giant's hallway. It had some really funky stalactites – they're the downward pointing ones, right?

This cavern had dozens of confusing passages branching off, so we stopped to consult the map.

When new trainees come to our school, they all get a copy of the Angel Handbook. Somewhere in the first two chapters (has to be – that's as far as

I've read!), it says: "*It's better to travel hopefully than to arrive.*"

Well, until that stalactite moment, I'd been in my hopeful-travelling groove. Trudge, trudge, meet some dead kids, kill a demon, trudge, trudge. I was just too worried to even *think* about how our mission might end, so I'd been acting like we'd be slogging through Limbo in our bare feet for ever. So when I looked at the map, I practically had heart failure. The butterfly was flashing a hundred metres away from where we were standing.

We were a hundred metres from the Palace of Endless Night.

"Omigosh, we've found her!" I squeaked.

"Better keep it down now," Reuben advised in a whisper. "There could be guards."

If I ever run into Jessica Lightpath again, I'm going to ask her, how come, in Limbo, you just have to *name* something and it appears?

Tramp, tramp, tramp. The sound echoed on and on, spookily amplified by the underground acoustic; the mechanical, unstoppable marching boots of soldiers who aren't quite human. We literally couldn't tell if there were ten soldiers storming towards us through the dark, or ten thousand.

Then, like a horde of giant cockroaches, they erupted from every passageway. There weren't ten thousand, but there were *definitely* more than ten, their dull black armour adding unpleasantly to the cockroach impression.

I'm not SO great at angelic martial arts, but I'm improving. Reuben, however, has got every heavenly belt going. He's like the teenage don of martial arts. But in normal life, neither one of us is capable of taking on a hundred-plus soldiers and leaving them in piles like laundry. Yet this is what happened.

It was like the peach stone episode only a zillion times more spectacular. We didn't have to think, we didn't have to go in a huddle about strategy. We went into total fight mode. We slammed into that dark lord's posse as if we'd been taking on armies our whole lives. We somersaulted off walls. We flew through the air like wire fighters (with no wires, might I add), and the soldiers went crashing down like skittles.

Once again I seemed to be split into two. The normal Mel was going; what the sassafras is going on! The wannabe-wire-fighter Mel was going; who cares? It's SO unbelievably cool!

My buddy and I fought our way all the way to the palace gates. The few guards on duty put up some resistance, but nothing we couldn't handle.

"We showed them," said Reuben, very slightly out of breath. "And the gates are open, excellent."

And then we clocked the building on the other side. Until this moment, it hadn't occurred to me that anyone would *choose* to build their palace out of stinky river mud, bits of skull and bone, and icky little plant organisms. Did I mention the gruesome gargoyle faces peering at us from inside tangles of living plant fibre, like old ladies snooping through net curtains? Did I also mention there were NO windows, anywhere?

I was dangerously close to another cosmic panic attack, when Reuben suddenly said this really helpful thing. "Just think, people all over the Universe must be taking deep breaths at this exact moment, as they psyche themselves up to do some scary but totally necessary thing."

I swallowed. Rescuing a human soul from a creepy palace in the underworld was hideously scary, but it made me feel heaps better to remember we weren't alone.

"If anyone asks, we're style consultants who've come to give them a makeover!" I said bravely.

And like other scared people all over the Universe, we took deep breaths, then walked through the gates and into the palace.

Eek, this style consultant just quit, I thought. My nostrils filled with an overwhelming mushroomy pong of mould and decay.

The dark lord's palace wasn't exactly welcoming from the outside, but the interior made me feel seriously deranged. First because it had all this creepy underground plant life growing *inside.*

Second, the palace was terminally confusing; stairs which stopped halfway to nowhere, dank corridors that constantly looped back on themselves. My worst thing was the swaying bridges, which initially appeared to take you to one part of the palace, yet infallibly delivered you in the opposite direction! After we'd found ourselves back by the front door for the squillionth time, Reuben suggested it might be better to ignore our physical surroundings.

"Keep your eyes on the map," he advised. "The butterfly will let us know if we're hot or cold."

"I'm so glad you're here, Reubs," I said impulsively. "I don't think I could have handled this by myself."

Reubs looked surprised. "Yeah, you could."

I shook my head. "I have these major cosmic wobbles, but when you're with me, I somehow keep it together."

"Works both ways, you know, Beeby," he pointed out.

I was amazed. "Really?"

"Yes, really. Now focus," he said sternly.

Reuben's strategy worked. By concentrating carefully on the dancing butterfly, we gradually made our way through the underground maze. At last a narrow twisty corridor brought us to the top of some cellar stairs. We stared down thoughtfully. Though every bit as dark and creepy as other stairs we'd seen, I noticed that these seemed much newer, as if they had been built more recently.

I felt a zing of angel electricity, and knew my hunch was right. Tsubomi's soul was down there! We didn't say a word. We just flew down the stairs.

The door at the bottom was locked. Reuben kicked it down with the same surprising strength he'd shown when he snapped the demon's torch.

Her vibes still hung in the air like a faint perfume. But Tsubomi's soul had gone.

Reuben shook his head. "It stinks of magic in here. The creep must have seen us coming and spirited her away somewhere."

I couldn't speak. I wandered about, stupidly picking up objects she might have touched and putting them down again.

I'm not into that "I live in a creepy church crypt" look, personally, and probably Tsubomi wasn't either, but you could see little human touches where she'd tried to make her underworld pad a bit more homey.

There was a sleeping area, divided by a lacquered screen, with a futon and a folded quilt. In her living area, Tsubomi had carefully arranged her art materials at one end of a low table; ink, parchment, various brushes. It looked like she'd been practising calligraphy to pass the time. At the opposite end of the table was a bowl of fresh strawberries. In the eerie twilight of the palace, their colours glowed like jewels.

There were real jewels too, spilling out of a casket; a tangle of bangles, chains and necklaces, in such disturbing designs they could only be gifts from the dark lord himself.

"WHY DID YOU COME?"

Dust rained down from the rocky ceiling. I clutched at Reubs, but by that time, the dark lord himself was towering over us, and anyway, there was nowhere to run.

"WHY DID YOU COME?"

"WHY DID YOU COME?"

"WHY DID YOU COME?"

Let me tell you, worn by a scary demon lord, the dull black armour of his soldiers absolutely did not make you think of cockroaches. It made him look exactly what he was, a terrifying samurai with evil powers. Each time he bellowed his question, he popped up in a different part of the room. This made it seem like there were several demon samurai bellowing at us simultaneously. As if one wasn't enough.

"What have you done with her soul, you monster?" I screamed to an empty space where he'd been standing seconds before.

More dust pattered down from the roof. This time there were actual stones and chunks of rock. I saw a little brown mouse skitter for cover.

"You dare to call ME a monster!" the dark lord thundered. "I SAVED Tsubomi. She had been too long in your world of Light. Her life had become shallow and one-dimensional. It was making her sick. She needed the richly textured darkness of the earth."

Richly textured poo, I thought. This lord obviously fancied himself as a bit of an intellectual.

The demon was pacing now. "I brought her to my palace," he said, slightly less thunderously. "I had this chamber built especially. I was going to educate her."

"What about? Darkness and dirt?" I whispered to Reubs.

"Tsubomi's mind was filled with trivia. She had forgotten humans are made of earth, as well as stardust. I saw past her ignorance. I was willing to work with her."

I suppressed a frightened squeak as the demon materialised an inch from my nose.

"She was afraid at first," he boomed. "But I expected that. I was hoping to convince her that I was her teacher, not her jailer, perhaps even something more."

"Something more?" I gulped.

"Lately she had shown signs of beginning to care for me. I brought her fruit and flowers from the world above. I gave her jewels."

He thrust his huge helmet close to my face. "And you Children of Light had to come and ruin everything!" he roared.

Reuben quickly placed himself between us. "Don't threaten her, man!" he said angrily. "We Children of Light stick together."

I was shaking like a rabbit. I'd had a good squint inside that helmet, and the creature inside was literally made of shadows. *Lucky Reuben's got that special dagger*, I thought.

"You didn't answer Mel's question." Reuben had taken up a martial-arts crouch. "What have you done with Tsubomi's soul?"

"Alas! I was weak!" The demon's boots made a hollow clumping sound as he paced. "We'd spent all those evenings together, listening to classical music."

Reuben gave me a comical look, like: "Eh?"

"I somehow couldn't bring myself to—" The dark lord was half talking to himself. He gave us a sudden malevolent glower. "Never fear! I shall have no such problem with you!"

"Be quick then, old man!" My buddy slid Heart Seeker out of his belt, lunging at the demon's chest. Nothing happened.

The dark lord howled with laughter. "You will not find what you seek inside this armour! Many have tried and ALL have failed!"

Still laughing, the dark lord slowly rose off the ground. Inhuman laughter rang out from the rocky walls and the earth beneath our feet.

I was practically wetting myself. Like Reubs, I'd been relying on the dagger. Now we were totally stuffed. "How do you kill something like that?" I whimpered to myself.

For absolutely no reason my eye was drawn to the table where Tsubomi had been practising calligraphy with ink and brushes.

Guess what?

That clever girl had written us a note! In beautiful calligraphy, she had copied out four lines of what looked like deep song lyrics, but which contained the exact answer to my question.

If you can't find the heart
in the darkness, babe,
try looking for the darkness
in the heart.

No, normally I wouldn't understand it either! But I was in Limbo mode, so I instantly caught on to what she was telling us. It was useless to look for the dark lord's heart inside his armour, because (euw euw euw!) he kept it SOMEWHERE ELSE. Believe it or not, I knew *exactly* where!

Reuben and the demon lord continued to whirl around the room, knocking over furniture.

I sidled over to Tsubomi's jewellery box and had a stealthy rummage among her collection of underworld knick-knacks. These included earrings carved out of what looked like coal, and a gruesome little charm bracelet hung with teeny skulls. The hideous locket was at the very bottom of the heap; a totally tasteless ruby-encrusted heart with a tiny see-through window. I didn't examine it TOO closely, but the twitching thing inside looked small enough, and *easily* dark enough, to be a dark lord's heart.

"Dagger please," I called calmly, like a nurse in *ER*.

My angel colleague immediately sent Heart Seeker spinning through the air. It made a sound like a v. sinister Frisbee. *Pyu. Pyu.*

The demon roared out a warning, but I'd already caught the dagger and plunged it through the locket, into the pulsing stuff inside.

The dark lord collapsed on to his knees with a yowl of pain that seemed to come from the core of the mountain itself.

Then he crashed to the floor and lay totally still. Strange-coloured steam rose, hissing faintly, from his armour. The dark lord had finally gone wherever dark lords go.

"No more abducting for you," my buddy told the steaming metal.

I was beside myself. "I am SO stupid. I killed him and we don't even know what he's done to her!"

Reuben pointed silently to the table. For the first time I noticed the litter of tiny green strawberry stalks and hulls beside the fruit bowl.

"Omigosh!" I wailed. "Doesn't she have *any* sense?"

"Don't blame Tsubomi. She had eaten nothing since she came to the palace."

For a moment I genuinely believed I was hallucinating. A v. small mouse was talking to us. It wasn't even talking in the special language angels use for communicating with animals. It was squeaking in medieval Japanese!

"Tonight the demon brought her a bowl of strawberries. She was so hungry and thirsty,

she'd eaten half the bowl before she realised what she was doing."

"That's helpful, little buddy, thanks," Reuben said politely. "Isn't there a fairy tale or something like this?" he asked.

"Cinderella had talking mice," I gulped. "In the Disney version."

"No, I meant the fruit. The girl ate an apple or a pomegranate or something, so she had to stay in the underworld for ev—"

Reuben never finished his sentence. There was a chime of music from some magical source. The palace dissolved around us, and we found ourselves in a totally different world.

CHAPTER SIX

My buddy and I were lying under a tree, head to head, exactly like before. The sky above was lit with an angry red glow.

"Woo! Serious *déjà vu!*"

I could feel Reuben's voice buzzing through my skull bones.

"Serious, *serious, déjà vu*," I agreed.

We scrambled to our feet and Reubs gave a low whistle.

"Now *that* is you!"

"How on earth can you tell?" I giggled.

We were completely dressed in black. Black hoods, loose black fighting clothes, black boots.

Even the lower parts of our faces were covered with black scarves.

"Hmm, first peasants, then ninjas," I mused aloud.

"Ninjas were like secret agents and assassins, right?" Reuben asked.

"Something like that."

There was some weirdly familiar logic behind this unexpected upgrade, but though I was racking my brains, I just could *not* remember what it was.

We were in a woodland glade almost identical to the first, but with crucial differences. The first glade had been lush and summery; here, dead and dying leaves floated down through the air, collecting in rustling drifts. Several trees seemed badly burned, either by lightning, forest fire or both. You could see their pale dead insides where the charred bark had peeled away. Somewhere beyond the fire-damaged trees, a wolf gave its lonely howl.

This world wasn't so pretty but it was *humongously* atmospheric!

Once again I felt like I'd fallen into an old Japanese painting. This one was totally painted in fire colours. Fiery red skies. Red dirt. Red and gold leaves.

"What would this poem say?" I wondered aloud.

Reuben looked blank. "Poem?"

"Japanese artists used to paint nature scenes to show the different seasons. Sometimes they'd write little haiku or whatever, to sum up the mood. Like if I wrote a poem about this wood, it might say something like..." I shut my eyes for a moment, then recited:

"*Summer came too soon.*

Flowers shrivel with a young girl's hopes

turning to smoke and ashes."

Reuben looked amazed. "You never told me you wrote poetry, Beeby!"

"I don't," I said. "Except when they made us at school."

I felt a bit weird about it, to be honest, so I hastily changed the subject. "Have you noticed this world smells different?"

The first wood had smelled of earth and rain. This one gave off a hot rubbery tang as if it hadn't rained in a thousand years.

A v. disturbing theory was forming at the back of my mind. A theory which totally explained all the things that made absolutely no sense otherwise; for example, how Reubs and I were able to mash up an entire army without getting a teeny scratch ourselves.

When I spotted the satchel hanging in the tree, I knew for sure my theory was right. I unhooked the new bag of Limbo goodies from the branch. This one was made from *way* better-quality leather. Without saying a word, I emptied the bag on to the ground. This is what was inside:

- One coil of rope with a useful hooky thing on the end.
- Two star-shaped ninja weapons.
- Small spiky objects for scaling high walls.
- One pristine new scroll.

I waved it triumphantly. "Ta-daa! I *knew* they'd give us a new map!"

Reuben gave me a severe look. "Mind telling me what's going on?"

"I'm not sure." I took a breath. "This might sound mad, but I think we're playing some kind of game."

"A game?" Reubs echoed.

"You know those musical chords we heard a few minutes ago? That's because we just went up a level. When we killed the dark lord, we absorbed his powers, which is why we've got more energy. I have, anyway."

"Yep, that sounds mad," he agreed.

"Because you never lived on Earth, hon! And you've never been interested in computer games. You said yourself this is like a fairy tale. Well, computer games are like interactive fairy tales. If you defeat the baddies you go up to the next level. If not, you lose a life and have to start again—"

My buddy held up his hand. "I'm lost. How can a world be a game?"

I shrugged. "It's just the only explanation that makes sense."

"To you," he said darkly.

"Remember the way things happened in that first world? How that kid gave you the dagger *after* we'd killed the first demon. That's exactly like a game. You have to earn things in games."

"I still don't—"

"OK, OK, how about the way we took out those soldiers? Remember the sound FX?"

He chuckled. "*Biff-boff*. I thought that was weird at the time."

"And those flying peach stones. *Zoom-zoom!*"

Reuben gave me a sideways grin. "The peach stones were cool!"

"*Très* cool," I agreed. "But they weren't *normal*."

"Not even for Limbo?" he asked wistfully.

I shook my head. "Sorry, Sweetpea."

I could see him gradually processing this new idea. "That would explain the birds," he admitted. "And you're right. I've got heaps more energy."

"Because we just went up a level. If you notice, everything is extra vibey."

"Extra vibey but still deeply sad."

My buddy unfurled our superior Level-Two scroll. I heard his sharp intake of breath. "Look who's back," he said huskily.

When I saw that little blue butterfly, I almost burst into tears. Our unexpected upgrade hadn't given me time to dwell on what the dark lord had done to Tsubomi. But she was OK, she was still OK!

"I can't believe it!" I said shakily. "She must have come up with us somehow after we killed the dark lord. From how he was talking, I thought he'd done something hideous to her."

Reubs frowned. "Supposing your game theory is right, who are we playing *against* exactly?"

I shook my head. "You're really trying to outwit the actual game itself. Plus you're trying to beat your own best efforts. I just hope we get to Tsubomi *before* the demon lord this time."

"The one on Level Two will be stronger, right?"

"Yeah, but we're stronger too, don't forget! Plus we've probably got heaps of cunning ninja skills we don't know about!" I grinned at him. Thanks for the TLC. Now these angel assassins had better hit the road!"

He laughed. "'Angel Assassins', sounds like the kind of hardcore stuff Brice listens to."

With Reuben improvising mad Angel-Assassin-type lyrics to make me laugh, we set off in the direction indicated by the butterfly.

Level Two was mountain country, rocky and arid. Nothing seemed to grow there except cacti and scrub, and the occasional pine tree. All the trees had been blasted by lightning along the exact same side. On Level Two peasant girls were clearing stones from the parched red fields, passing filled baskets to each other in a never-ending chain gang, and the ladies who rode past in creaky wicker carriages were fluttering their fans to keep cool, not just for coyness purposes.

In its own way, Level Two was fabulously scenic.

At intervals we'd glimpse fairy-tale castles perched on rocky ledges high above the track.

"Noticed how every castle comes with an identical pine tree?" Reuben commented.

"Yeah, yeah and the birds always fly in sevens!"

"These are eagles," he grinned. "They mostly fly solo."

I looked up and sure enough there was exactly one fierce golden-brown eagle soaring on a current of hot air. "Boy, you really notice every tiny thing!" I marvelled.

We were practically jogging by this time, easily overtaking yet another travelling harp player.

や あ yā "Hi," we said in medieval Japanese.

や あ yā "Hi," he answered politely.

On Level Two, the musicians wore scarves tied over their mouths, bandit-style, to keep out the dust.

We passed so many harp players, not to mention woodcutters and travelling monks, that I had a strong suspicion some of them were ninjas in disguise.

I was starting to think like a ninja by this time! I'm serious! Suddenly my mind was totally humming with devious strategies; scanning the mountainside for caves to hide out in, bushes to skulk behind, castles to raid. I had no intention of raiding a castle for real, obviously, but if I HAD wanted to, I had all the relevant ninja skills at my fingertips.

"See that castle?" I called to my ninja angel buddy, as we jogged on under glowing skies. "If we crawled through those bushes, we'd find a secret ninja path that would lead us right into the lord's private chamber, without the soldiers even seeing!"

"Yeah, but the lord of the castle would be expecting us," Reuben pointed out. "He'll have spent a fortune making it ninja-proof; secret entrances, hidden stairways, floors that sing like canaries when you step on the wrong board!"

I grinned. "It's cool knowing all this stuff isn't it!"

"Seriously cool," he agreed.

We had gradually increased our pace, until we were literally running. I'm not a great fan of running normally, but on Level Two it felt really natural.

The landscape was becoming increasingly otherworldly. Lone lightning-struck trees were replaced by strange Martian-looking rocks.

"Some of this rock looks volcanic," Reuben said, when we stopped to check the map.

"I haven't seen any volcanoes!"

My buddy pointed into the distance.

Me and my big mouth, I thought.

A v. ominous cone-shaped mountain loomed on the horizon. Plumes of smoke belched out, in that unsubtle way you see in cartoons. When you are a complete wuss, even a cartoon volcano is enough to scare you silly. I swallowed, and for the second time that day, I heard a wolf howl close by. Reuben saw my face.

"Wolves don't hurt people," he reassured me. "That's just a myth."

He went back to studying the map. "This butterfly is zigzagging all over the place!" he complained. "Last time I looked it was off to the side. Now it's behind us." He tugged at his dreads in frustration. "Mel, I hate to say this, but I think Tsubomi's stalking *us*."

I gasped. "You're kidding!"

Neither of us had the least idea what you did if the lost soul reversed cosmic protocol and started following you!

I blew a dusty strand of hair out of my eyes. "The first challenge was to do with earth," I said slowly. "This level has to be about fire, so presumably our second-level challenge is to do with fire too."

Reuben gestured to the smoking mountain. "Things don't get much more fiery than that."

"I suppose we could head in that direction for a while, and see if Tsubomi follows? Unless you've got a better idea?" I said hopefully.

He hadn't. Luckily it's impossible to worry and run simultaneously. Perhaps because running in this world felt SO exhilarating. At times it felt like we were standing still and it was the landscape flying past!

This is how a leopard feels, I thought, racing across the savannah, with the wind rushing through its fur.

From time to time I heard a wolf give that lonely full-throated howl. Like, "YAROO!" At times it seemed worryingly close. Other times it sounded echoey and far away.

The sun was low on the horizon when we both skidded to a halt.

We stared down at the fresh paw prints in the dust.

Reuben shook his head. "That wolf is following us!"

Everyone was following us, if you asked me. Lost souls, wolves. There was probably an entire army of ninja assassins trailing us through the undergrowth at this moment.

"I thought you said wolves were harmless."

He pulled a face. "In Limbo, who knows? We should probably camp here. It'll be freezing, because there's absolutely no shelter, but if anything IS trying to creep up on us, we'd see it for miles."

Reuben was thinking like a ninja too.

We lit a fire, in case the lone wolf turned out to be a scout for a ravening pack. Then we wrapped ourselves in our cloaks and watched the sunset. Level Two sunsets are *totally* fabulous. When darkness came it had a faint red glow.

My stomach gave a long rumble.

"Hungry?" asked Reuben.

"I'd even eat trail mix," I said gloomily.

I unrolled the map to check on Tsubomi's position.

The butterfly had vanished.

"That's impossible!" said Reuben in dismay. "I looked ten minutes ago and she was right *here*!"

"Are you looking for me?"

A ninja girl stepped out from the shadows. She wore a shabby cloak over her baggy fighting clothes, and there was a stringed instrument slung over her shoulder. Like me and Reubs, Tsubomi's soul had put on a Limbo disguise, but I recognised her instantly.

"Omigosh! We *found* you!"

"Erm, excuse me!" she laughed. "It was actually me who found you!"

Tsubomi sounded just like she did in the Agency documentary. Cool, sassy, yet oddly grown-up.

"I've been hoping we'd hook up eventually. I wanted to thank you for taking out the dark lord," she grinned.

"You *knew* about that?" Reuben said amazed.

She seemed surprised. "Of course! You both did a brilliant job!"

"Only because you left that note," I said modestly. "It was really a team effort."

Tsubomi shuddered. "Can you imagine anything so gross! Actually giving someone your *heart* in a locket!"

"If you think about it, it was a HUGE compliment!" I told her quickly. "The dark lord must have liked you a lot. He was literally putting his life in your hands."

Stop babbling, babe, I told myself.

It was partly stage fright at finding myself chatting to a real celebrity. But mostly it was because I'd always imagined this would be the easy bit. And I'd just realised that having finally found our human, we didn't have a clue what to do next!

"Well," I said brightly. "I guess we should get you back to your—"

I couldn't finish my sentence. I had a chilling flash of that dying girl wired up to those machines and, I'm sorry, I just could NOT bring myself to say the word, "body".

"—back home," I said huskily. "We'll get you back home, in a trice. You probably won't even know you've been away."

Tsubomi laughed. "That would be lovely – if I had a home to go back to! Sadly I don't. For now this world is my home, and I have a really difficult task to carry out."

Jessica had told us that lost souls often have the strangest delusions about why they're in Limbo.

"Gosh! What kind of task?" I asked, to humour her. "Like a quest you mean?"

"Maybe I'll tell you tomorrow," she said evasively. "Is it OK if I stay with you guys till morning?"

"We'd like that." My buddy suddenly looked hopeful. "Any chance I can have a strum on that – is it a lute?"

"It's called a koto," I corrected.

Tsubomi laughed. "Actually a koto would be way too big and bulky to carry around. You call this a 'biwa'. Reuben's right, it's a sort of lute. Play it by all means." She added carelessly, "I don't actually know why I'm lugging it around. It's not like I'm a musician or anything."

"So you don't play yourself?" he asked.

She shrugged. "Everyone plays a bit, don't they?"

"Not really," I began.

Reuben gave me a look, and, remembering the sacred rules of soul-retrieval: *we wait, we watch, we keep our gobs shut,* I hastily shut mine.

Be patient, I told myself. Maybe that miracle will happen like Jessica said, and Tsubomi will remember who she is.

Level Two might be a simmering dust bowl during the day, but it gets FREEZING when the sun goes down. I was really grateful for that campfire.

Tsubomi was holding out her hands to the flames. Suddenly she cleared her throat. "You've been really kind and I feel like I owe it to you to tell you the truth. The problem is, I know it's going to change the way you feel about me."

I felt like *such* a pro! We'd only known her ten minutes, yet already Tsubomi trusted us enough to spill the beans about the stresses and strains that had driven her to take her accidental overdose.

"Don't tell us unless you really want to," I said in my gentlest voice.

She swallowed. "It's about the dark lord."

My smile froze on my face. "Oh, right."

"He told you he couldn't bring himself to kill me. What he didn't tell you, is when I ate the fruit, I immediately fell under an evil curse."

"Omigosh," I said. "You poor thing! What kind of curse?"

"I'm only a girl by night," Tsubomi said earnestly. "But when the sun rises, I have to take on the shape of a wolf."

"You're kidding!" I breathed.

She giggled. "How do you think I crept up on you earlier? Ninja skills? Yeah right! Wolves can outsmart ninjas every time!"

"But that's so awful," I said in horror. "How can you joke about it?"

Tsubomi shook her head. "It's not *so* bad. It's taught me a lot actually."

Tsubomi was surprisingly eager to talk about her wolf experiences. After several long and extremely detailed descriptions of fascinating smells (fascinating to a wolf that is), Reubs and I got a bit restless. We kept tactfully trying to bring the conversation round to Tsubomi's real life in Japan; her home, her studies, parents and friends. But we just hit this total wall.

To hear her talk, you'd have thought she'd been *born* inside this game. I can see why. It might be weird and scary but it was also extremely simple. Inside the game, Tsubomi didn't have to stress about her mother, or her agent, her fans or promoters. She didn't have to jump on and off planes, zooming from one city to another, meeting ridiculous schedules. She was as free as, well, a wolf.

Reuben was tinkering softly with the harp. He asked Tsubomi to show him how to tune it properly. I watched her lively laughing face as she corrected his fingering, and shut my eyes to banish the chilling image of the blank girl lying in a hospital bed.

I could literally feel the minutes ticking, ticking. For souls who've left their bodies for keeps, time obviously doesn't present a problem. But each minute, each *second* Tsubomi Hoshi's soul spent in Limbo made it increasingly unlikely she would ever be able to return to life on Earth.

Reuben seemed totally oblivious. He'd started playing a funky old-style Japanese version of one of his own songs. I got the impression Tsubomi was having some kind of internal struggle with herself. Finally, she couldn't resist, she started to sing along. The evening turned into an impromptu jam session. Sometimes Tsubomi sang, sometimes Reuben, sometimes they sang together. Like I said, Reubs doesn't have what you'd call a great voice, but their voices harmonised beautifully.

It's not unusual for me to have at least two Melanies squabbling inside my head at any one time, but suddenly there was an entire football team! Mel Number One was stressing about how we were going to save Tsubomi. Mel Number Two, I'm ashamed to tell you, was hopping with jealousy! Reuben was my angel buddy. And Tsubomi and I had a special soul connection from who knows where. So how come *I* was the cosmic gooseberry?

Mel Number Three ached with pure envy. If I could only open my mouth and have a wonderful sound come out, instead of a tuneless squeak. Mel Number Four on the other hand...

Fortunately, I eventually ran out of Melanies, and just dozed uneasily against the rocks. I was woken by the sound of Reuben stamping on the remains of our fire.

The sun was coming up over the mountains like a huge gold beach ball.

My buddy beamed at me. "You're awake! Great evening wasn't it?"

"Yeah. Great!" I agreed brightly.

He looked worried. "Do you think it was a bad idea, getting her to play? I hoped playing music might remind her. But she's got a huge block about it. Like she wants to play, but she thinks she shouldn't. I'm worried I just made her even more confused."

"Oh, I'm sure you didn't," I started.

"She just kept bringing everything back to this task, or quest, or whatever. It's like she thinks she's some character in a fairy tale."

"You noticed that too." I was brushing red dust off my ninja clothes.

I felt like such a child. Reuben hadn't been trying to leave me out. He'd been doing his job. *Like you should be doing, Mel,* I scolded myself.

"Where is she this morning?" I asked guiltily.

"Up on those rocks," Reuben said in a low voice. "Keep your voice down, she's quite jumpy."

A young she-wolf was eying us nervously from the rocks.

Tsubomi must have changed back at sunrise. I was so ashamed of myself, I can't tell you. What kind of angel is *jealous* of the soul she came to save?

Reuben has this unnerving way of reading my mind. "Don't feel too sorry for her," he said, carefully folding up his cloak. "In some weird way, I think this is actually doing Tsubomi good."

"You think being under a curse is doing her *good*? Is that, like, Level Two logic!"

"Don't twist my words, Beeby," he said mildly. "I meant being a wolf. Running on all fours, exposed to the elements, sniffing all those smells. The dark lord had a point. This has to be healthier than that life she had before."

"I never thought about it like that," I admitted.

"Jessica's right. We've just got to go along with this big quest delusion, let Tsubomi run with it and see where it goes."

"Oh," I gulped. "I was thinking the exact opposite."

"I could tell," he said gently. "But I think we should hang on in."

"She's *dying*, Reubs."

"I know, but if we interfere, we're disrespecting her, don't you see? If we want to save her, we have to trust her, even when she's doing something that seems crazy or dangerous."

I was close to tears. "It's just the hardest thing I've ever done."

Reuben patted my back. "Me too, and we should probably get going."

I tried to grin. "Yeah, Fido's getting restless!"

Up on the mountainside, a bored Tsubomi was chasing her tail.

She followed us all the rest of that day as we covered the remaining miles to the volcano. I say "followed", but it's more like she roamed around us in huge circles, like a hyperactive puppy.

As we got nearer, something happened that is really not easy to put into words. Something started calling to us. Not in words, like a force, some fierce fabulous attraction that tugged ruthlessly at our heartstrings, drawing us closer and closer and closer...

This probably sounds v. alarming, so you'll have to believe me when I say that it *felt* wonderful! We'd been travelling for hours, yet not only were we not tired, Reubs and I were just bubbling with high spirits; laughing, teasing each other, doing silly walks. It was like we were actually being energised by our proximity to the volcano.

"This feels like falling in love," Reuben said, half laughing at himself.

"True love on an industrial scale!" I agreed.

It was evening by the time we reached the lower slopes.

The track snaked around a sharp bend and suddenly, high above us, was the most magical-looking palace. Its walls had been covered in millions of pieces of highly polished metal. Each one reflected the setting sun, turning the palace into one huge blazing mirror.

Then I realised. The sun had already set. The light wasn't a reflection, it was flooding out from inside. The palace must be the source of the humongous life force we'd felt zinging from every stone and tiny desert plant. I could actually see it, now, radiating out from the palace, looking exactly like the sunrays baby angels like to put in their paintings.

"This is the Palace of Eternal Flames. It's even

more amazing than I imagined!" Tsubomi appeared, babbling with excitement.

Angels are used to high levels of cosmic energy, and the extraordinary volcano vibes had *us* buzzing. Tsubomi was as high as a kite! Gabbling on about how she knew we were really her friends, how special last night was, sharing our fire and our companionship. But to cut a long, l-o-n-g story short, Tsubomi had finally decided she could trust us. "I'm going to tell you absolutely everything," she told us.

We'd committed ourselves to going along with Tsubomi's quest fantasy as you know. Jessica would expect us to follow her soul into the boiling crater of the volcano if necessary. I'm not sure if she'd have wanted us to commit actual burglary though. My heart sank into my ninja boots, as Tsubomi explained exactly how she'd break into the Palace of Eternal Flames and steal its owner's most treasured possession.

"Oh, and I want you both to come with me," she bubbled. "It's going to be totally thrilling. Back in a sec, I'm just going to scout around and check out the positions of the guards."

More like she just can't sit still, I thought gloomily.

I let her get out of earshot, then told Reubs how I felt.

"I know it's just a game, but something in that palace has real power, and I don't think Tsubomi has a clue what she's getting into."

"I agree," he said quietly, "but we agreed we had to trust her."

"Reubs, she's planning to go storming up a volcano, and rob some scary fire demon of – of who knows *what*? She thinks this is just some fairy tale, and she can't get hurt. She's never even asked herself, 'Hello! Where did this robbery idea come from? Who ARE these demon lords?'"

Reuben sounded disturbed. "I assumed they were a game thing."

"So did I. But now I'm thinking, who set this game up? Who's making the rules?"

My buddy swallowed. We both knew I was talking about the PODS.

He dropped his voice. "You're worried this is a trap?"

I nodded. "And we could be helping her walk right into it."

We heard an owl hoot, not very convincingly.

Tsubomi appeared, looking delighted with herself. "Are you guys ready? I needn't have panicked about the moat. I know *exactly* how we're going to get in."

To my surprise, the first part of the operation went really smoothly. In fact, considering Reuben and I had only been ninjas for twenty-four hours max, it was a breeze! I could see why Tsubomi had been worried about the moat. (Instead of scuzzy water, it was full of boiling lava.) But with the help of the cunning hooked rope from our bag of Limbo resources, not to mention our ninja throwing skills, we calmly abseiled over it.

The shiny mirror walls of the Fire Palace presented more of a problem. Then yours truly remembered the little spiky things in our bag. They were really cunning, actually. We whacked them on to our boots and just ran up the shiny mirror walls of the palace like flies, until we reached an open window. We climbed in, removed spikes and boots, and crept down the glowing gleaming corridors in our padded socks, as quietly as cats.

OK, the first time flames spurted out of the floor at my feet, I might have let out a teensy squeak of surprise, but once you got into the rhythm, (pad, pad, pad, spurt of fire, pad, pad, pad) it was easy.

Now and then guards would erupt from a doorway and we'd do some serious biffing and boffing. These soldiers wore red armour, the dull red of smouldering coals. And they had these staffs that sent out splurts of pure lightning. Luckily we moved so fast, they didn't get much use out of them.

Our ninja fighting stars were *très* cool. If you threw them with just the right amount of spin, (*pyu, pyu*) you could take out three or four guards at once. But mostly we stuck to old-fashioned biffing and boffing. Leaving a trail of stunned, silent bodies, we fought our way to a huge door framed by carved pillars. The energy coming from inside was so strong; I could literally feel it buzzing in the roots of my teeth.

What the sassafras is in there? I thought nervously.

Like the outer walls, the door was made from tiny pieces of bright hammered metal. In the shining mirrored surface, the ghosts of flames flickered and flared.

Tsubomi listened carefully at the door, with that expression you see on safe-crackers on TV. "It's still sleeping. Good," she whispered to herself. She took a hairpin out of her hair and began jiggling the lock. I heard a spring give inside. Next, she took a feather and a small bottle from her bag and softly oiled the hinge. Only then did she risk turning the handle.

The door swung open as smooth as butter.

I don't know what I expected on the other side, but it definitely wasn't a glowing fire garden with red, gold and rose-coloured flames for flowers. In the centre of the garden, where normal people might have a water feature, the demon had a fountain – of *fire*.

In the white-hot heart of the fountain, was the most magical bird I have ever seen. She had glittering gold-tipped feathers and flaming sunset colours on her breast. She seemed peacefully asleep, her wings carefully spread over her clutch of eggs. I couldn't see them properly, but I glimpsed soft gleams of colour.

"Either I'm dreaming," breathed Reuben, "or that's a real phoenix."

Tsubomi smothered a nervy giggle. "Of course it's a phoenix. It's the source of the fire demon's power," she mused. "Don't feel bad about her eggs, we're only taking one."

Reuben was absolutely appalled. "You don't seriously intend to steal a phoenix egg!"

I saw the phoenix open an amber-yellow eye. *Oh-oh*, I thought.

"It's my task," Tsubomi said in her fairy-tale voice. "I thought you and Melanie understood that."

The phoenix stirred, clearly uneasy. A loose feather floated from her fiery nest, brushing Tsubomi's cheek. I saw a bright red weal appear. Somehow she managed not to cry out. The shock made tears well in her eyes.

"I thought I'd know," she whispered. "I thought I'd know what to do, when we got to the palace, but I don't."

It would have been better, obviously, if she could have told us this *before* she made us abseil over a moat filled with molten lava, but she looked so vulnerable, that I felt really sorry for her. Until that phoenix feather gave her a nasty burn, Tsubomi thought she was living inside a magical story where the hero isn't allowed to get hurt. Now she knew better.

"I brought you guys here, and I have no idea how we're even supposed to do this," she whispered, ashamed.

"That's OK," Reuben told her calmly. "Something will come to you."

I don't think it was his words, so much as the smile, that calmed her down. Lola calls it his "Sweetpea smile". She says when Reubs gives you that smile, you just know in your heart that everything in the Universe is totally cool.

Tsubomi's expression changed. Even the energy in the room changed. "I have to play my lute," she whispered. "I didn't realise, but I think it might actually be magic."

"Play it and see," Reuben suggested.

And be quick before Mama Phoenix loses any more of those scary feathers, I thought nervously. The phoenix was getting *really* restless.

Scared but determined, Tsubomi unstrapped her harp. It looked like a normal lute to me, as normal as a lute can look by the glowing light of a phoenix fire. I'm not sure that her agent would have approved of her singsong magic chant. But the phoenix *loved* it! She started making ecstatic cooing sounds.

"It is, it's a magic lute," Tsubomi breathed to herself, as if music was only OK if it was magic.

"Don't stop," Reuben hissed.

He was gradually edging over to the nest, suddenly he plunged his gloved hand into the flames and pulled out a phoenix egg.

"Go, go, go!" he urged.

Too late. The phoenix exploded out of her nest. A nanosecond later we all got the shock of our lives, as she morphed into a hideous scaly red demon with one blazing amber-yellow eye and more arms than is actually attractive.

I wasn't as scared as you might think. All you need to kill a fire demon is water, right?

"Have you got a bottle of water in that bag?" I screamed at Tsubomi.

She started emptying her bag frantically. "Nothing!" she screamed back. "Just a stupid peach stone."

Yess! Thank you!

I literally snatched it out of her hand.

I remember thinking, I'll only get one shot, I'd better do it right.

ZOOM. The peach stone skimmed towards the demon, hitting her smack in the eye, her yellow all-seeing eye. Crude, perhaps, cruel, definitely, but *extremely* effective!

While the female demon blundered around her magical fire garden, howling in pain and clutching her blinded eye, we fled from the palace. We made it back over the palace moat, in time to see the sun coming up. Reubs and I collapsed into each other's arms, almost hysterical with relief.

"Nice work, Beeby," he congratulated me.

"Hey, I'm just grateful Tsubomi had that peach stone!"

Tsubomi wasn't paying one scrap of attention to this conversation. "It's sunrise," she said in a stunned voice. "And I'm still a girl!"

I stared at her. "Omigosh, that is SO cool! The dark lord's curse must have been broken. Now you can go back to—"

My words were drowned by horribly familiar musical chords. Tsubomi vanished. A second later, so did Reuben.

I stood alone on the volcano, the hot wind whipping through my hair, waiting my turn to be whisked up to Level Three.

This isn't right, I thought. *Tsubomi got her phoenix egg. This game is over. The game lords or whoever can't just go on shuttling us from level to level like pinballs!*

My surroundings blurred out of focus. I heard a sound like wind chimes, or tiny temple bells. I tried to remember what came after earth and fire. A deadly chill crept into the soles of my feet and rose up my legs. Ice? Could that be right? Earth, fire… ICE?

CHAPTER SEVEN

The light was unbelievably bright. And my bum was *unbelievably* cold!

Seen from the air, we would have made a star shape. Three of us, lying head to head, our arms outstretched.

Icicles tinkled overhead, making the wind chime sound I'd heard as I switched levels. I scrambled to my feet. Same wood, totally different world. This world was pure white. Everywhere you looked, just pure sparkling white.

"Is this what snow is like?" My buddy's face was a picture of amazement.

"This IS snow, bird brain," I said affectionately.

"Ah, that's SO cute! I can't believe you never saw snow before!" I stooped down, stealthily packing my gloved hand with snow. "So, erm, I'm guessing you don't know about the sacred snow ritual?"

Reubs glanced up innocently. "What's that?"

I hurled the snowball, catching my shocked buddy bang on the nose.

Reuben wagged his finger. "OK, Beeby, now that was sad! You did that just like a girl!"

"Yeah? Don't remember you complaining when I saved your booty from the one-eyed fire demon!"

"We're talking about style," he said loftily. "But it's never too late to learn from the master. Now THIS is a stylish throw!"

Next minute the two of us were having a major snowball fight. We'd reached the childish stage of stuffing snow down each others necks, when I became aware of Tsubomi watching us, tapping an elegant boot on the frozen ground.

"Omigosh, look at YOU," I breathed.

"I'm not sure we should be wearing fur," Reuben said doubtfully.

We'd been upgraded to noble Japanese lords and ladies. All three of us wore padded, fur-trimmed winter robes, absolutely stiff with embroidery. My hair was in its usual messy style (it's basically untameable). Tsubomi's was carefully put up with combs. Underneath our outer robes, Tsubomi and I wore a number of gauzy inner robes in layers. Mine were pure winter tones, grey, ivory, silver, shimmery green; each colour peeping out from under the next.

"You wouldn't think dreads would go," I told Reuben admiringly, "but they look fab."

"Could we get started, everyone, please? We *are* supposed to be on a quest!" Tsubomi's tone was as cold as the weather.

I guiltily shook loose snow out of my robes, and hastily went into celestial-agent mode. "Has anyone seen a bag?" I asked them bossily. "There should be a bag of Limbo goodies around here somewhere."

"No, there's just this," Tsubomi said evasively.

I noticed she was clasping a large mother-of-pearl casket, bound with hoops of gold.

"Ohh, that's SO pretty! Have you opened it to see what's inside?"

"No, and I don't intend to. I'll just look after it until we need it," said Tsubomi in her new frosty voice.

I was hurt. On the last level we'd all been mates

together. Now suddenly Tsubomi was treating us like her minions or whatever.

We were all suddenly distracted by icy tinkling sounds.

Waiting for us under the trees were three milk-white horses, their saddles gorgeously decorated in medieval Japanese style. The bridles were hung with dozens of tiny silver bells, which jingled musically whenever they moved.

Woo, we are *going up in the world*, I thought.

As noble ladies, Tsubomi and I had to sit side-saddle. Tsubomi positioned the mysterious casket in front of her on her saddle. She kept darting uneasy looks in our direction.

"Does she think we're going to *steal* it?" I whispered to Reuben.

"Who knows what she's thinking?" he sighed. "I get the feeling she doesn't totally remember who we are."

"More like she totally doesn't care!" I muttered.

As if to prove my point, Tsubomi spurred her horse and cantered off, sending up flurries of powdery snow.

"Just out of interest, where are we going?" I called.

"I don't have to answer to you," she called back. "This is my quest. You just have to follow me and do what I say."

Reuben and I exchanged astounded looks.

"Do you think she's been talking to Jess Lightpath?" he joked.

"I think she's being a right little diva!"

Reuben watched a rapidly disappearing Tsubomi with concern. "Don't think your little diva is going to stop," he commented.

We galloped for ages before we finally caught her up. It was *très* exhilarating actually, riding through the sparkling winter landscape. The weight of so much snow had bent some trees totally down to the ground, so they formed a series of dazzling white archways. It was like riding through some hushed ice cathedral.

Until Reuben pointed it out, I didn't realise anything was missing.

"I haven't seen one single person," he said abruptly.

"Good," said Tsubomi in a sharp voice. "People are more trouble than they're worth."

"No, they're not," I snapped. Sorry, I was not in the mood for humouring snotty fairy-tale princesses today.

"I haven't even seen a bird," Reuben pondered. "You'd think there'd be birds, or squirrels or foxes. But there's just us."

A moment later we saw the musician, his fingers still poised on the strings of the battered biwa. Both the musician and his harp were totally encased in ice. Reubs and I slid off our horses and rushed to see if we could help.

"Can that happen?" I whispered. "Can someone be frozen stiff in the middle of playing the lute?"

We were going to try to thaw him with our vibes, but Tsubomi just went zooming off again, just as if absolutely nothing was wrong! By this time, we knew she was capable of just galloping on for ever, so we had to jump back on our horses and race after her. I really hated leaving that poor guy all alone in the snow.

Frozen musicians became a distressingly familiar sight. We also saw a number of frozen carriages abandoned at the side of the road. Ice crystals had transformed them into twinkling fairy-tale coaches. Each coach had a sorrowful Cinderella frozen inside. We rode on past woods and temples and roadside shrines, through a white, sparkling, silent world where everything and everyone had totally turned to ice.

Throughout this deeply harrowing journey, Tsubomi didn't say a word. She seemed more worried about the casket, giving it anxious little pats, as if to reassure herself it was still there.

I don't know why it took me so long to catch on. Maybe phoenix vibes are affected by the cold? But all at once I felt it, a tiny fiery whisper of the fabulous life force we'd felt on Level Two.

I manoeuvred my horse alongside Reuben's.

"Guess what's in the casket," I whispered.

"Can't," he whispered back.

"I just felt a teeny tiny phoenix vibe. She must have brought the egg from Level Two."

"Do you think she knows? What's inside the casket, I mean?"

I shook my head. "Just that it's precious. You notice she's guarding it like a Doberman?"

"It's like, on this level she knows and she doesn't know at the same time," he sighed. "Like she *half* remembers us, but she doesn't know if she can trust us."

"You think that's why she's acting so weird?" Seen in this light, Tsubomi's behaviour made a lot more sense.

"I get the feeling she remembers she's meant to do something special," Reuben explained. "She just has no idea what. The poor kid's totally lost. You can see it in her eyes."

Reuben has this amazing ability to see through to the basic goodness inside people, even when they're being anything but.

My eyes unexpectedly filled with tears. "Sweetpea, you're such a – such an *angel*."

"Meaning?"

"I see a diva with a bad attitude, you just see—" I shook my head, not quite trusting my voice. *A very scared human*, I thought.

It was obvious, now he'd pointed it out. I'd been so wrapped up in my own selfish feelings, I'd totally misread her behaviour.

With no map, no idea where we were going, and Tsubomi frostily refusing advice, our journey fell into a weird pattern. We'd ride like demons until we reached a crossroad, then wait around until she decided which road to take.

Riding in aimless circles in the snow, in pursuit of a lost soul who has no idea who she is or where she's supposed to be going, is a deeply overrated pastime. If it hadn't been for Jessica's insistence that this was the only way to save Tsubomi, I doubt we'd have had the nerve to stick with the programme.

The sun went down. There were no crossroads in sight, so we just rode on. The moon rose over the frozen trees, turning the road into a shimmery white ribbon.

"It's cold." They were the first words Tsubomi had spoken for hours. She shivered in her embroidered robes, looking like a haughty, but extremely frightened, royal child.

I decided it was time to drop a teeny cosmic hint.

"This might sound bizarre," I said cautiously, "but when I really REALLY don't know what to do, I sometimes just ask for help."

"Perhaps you didn't notice, but there isn't anyone to ask." Tsubomi's teeth were chattering. She sounded about six years old.

"That's why Melanie said it sounded bizarre," Reuben said softly.

"I don't even know what I'm doing here," Tsubomi said in that same scared, small voice. "I'm just so cold and tired."

It was a v. delicate moment. We aren't allowed to tell humans what to do. But inside, I'm going, *just* ask, *dammit! How can the Universe answer you if you don't even ASK?*

Tsubomi gave a hopeless shrug. "I'll try anything, if it will make this stop."

She shut her eyes. "If anyone's listening, please, please help me. I don't think I can do this on my own any more."

The horses slowed with a jingle of their harness. One of them whickered a greeting to someone standing under the trees. Then the moon came out from behind a cloud, and I saw the lady. She was standing in a shaft of pure moonlight. In her silvery robes, she looked almost as if she was made of moonlight herself.

Tsubomi gasped and slithered off her horse. She bowed several times, as if she knew this lady from somewhere, or had heard of her maybe.

"I am Lady Tsukii," the lady explained. "My house is just a few steps from here. You are welcome to shelter there for the night."

Reubs and I dismounted, and bowed to show respect. Our horses weren't in the least respectful! They were shamelessly nuzzling her sleeves, to see if she had anything interesting to eat.

Reuben whispered, "The horses obviously trust her. Tsubomi trusts her."

"And we can't exactly ride round all night," I whispered back.

Sorry, Jessica, I thought. *Even angels have to break rules sometimes.*

We followed the lady over a snowy footbridge, and through a sparkling winter garden. Instead of taking us straight to her house, Lady Tsukii led us to a special teahouse in the grounds. Snow lay so thickly on the roof, it literally looked quilted. The full moon hung overhead like a paper lantern drenching everything with its light.

Lady Tsukii poured water over our hands from a special pot, then we took off our shoes and ducked through the doorway.

The teahouse radiated such a sweet, still vibe I can't describe it. Everything was calm and simple. The low table and cushions, the floor mats giving off a faint smell of rushes, a spray of winter berries in a jar.

I had heard about Japanese tea ceremonies. I knew it wasn't going to be like at my mum's, where you just plonked in a Tetleys bag for a brew. But I had no idea it was so, you know, *deep.*

Each step was exact and perfect, like the flowing movements of a dance, as Lady Tsukii poured boiling water on to the tea leaves in the pot, whisked it to a green froth, then poured the liquid into an earthenware cup. She handed it to Tsubomi, and something in the way she did it, made this simple gesture seem truly meaningful.

Tsubomi turned the cup, once, twice, three times, before she lowered her face to drink. Like Lady Tsukii she was totally concentrating on what she was doing. She carefully wiped the rim with a snowy white napkin, then it was my turn.

As I took the cup, the lady's eyes met mine, and any doubts I had just melted away. She *knew*. She absolutely knew who we were. I felt it deep inside. Whoever she was, she had come to help Tsubomi just when she needed it most, and that's really all we needed to know.

I sipped at the hot green tea, taking my time, letting the peace and stillness of the teahouse flow into me.

By the time the ceremony was over, Tsubomi looked calmer than I'd ever seen her. Lady Tsukii led us back across the moonlit garden to her house. For a second time we removed our footwear and put on the slippers that were waiting on the other side of the sliding door.

Like the teahouse, Lady Tsukii's house was calm and simple inside – and blissfully warm! Opening up the stove, she carefully laid two sticks of incense on the glowing charcoal. A wonderful smell of sandalwood and frankincense filled the air (they used those oils all the time in ancient Rome), and other perfumes I couldn't identify.

Now we were indoors, I could see that the lady's robes were heavily embroidered with silver thread. This must have been what had given the shimmery moonlight effect. Yet that first mysterious impression remained. Just the way she moved totally mesmerised me. *It's not just the tea ceremony*, I thought. *She does every little thing like it matters.* I was sure I'd never met anyone like her, yet Lady Tsukii really reminded me of somebody. But for the life of me I couldn't think who.

Everything Lady Tsukii did was designed to make us feel like honoured guests. She provided us with beautiful kimonos to wear while our own robes dried overnight. Mine was a gorgeous, rich, plum colour – with a matching fan. She also brought us special nibbles; and all without hurry or fuss. When we were sitting comfortably on cushions, she indicated an ancient-looking koto (Tsubomi was right – it was too big to lug around), and invited Reuben to play. "I'll do my best," he said doubtfully. "I've only played a Japanese lute before and that just had four strings."

She smiled. "When you are a true musician, the number of strings does not really matter." Have you not heard of the master who played the most divine music ever heard on a koto with just one string?"

"I know that story!" Tsubomi's face lit up. "I could never understand how he did it!"

The lady's eyes held a mischievous sparkle. "Did you never think perhaps that legendary musician was a *she*?"

"That has to be it!" I joked. "My mum always said women have to do at least three impossible things before breakfast!"

After Reuben had done his party piece, the lady asked Tsubomi to play. She seemed so nervous that Lady Tsukii tactfully suggested singing an old folk song together. It was only when I saw them singing, side by side, that it clicked. Lady Tsukii was like Tsubomi! How Tsubomi could be, hopefully would be, when she was older and wiser.

If we save her, I thought. I felt a sudden ache in my throat.

"Your friend tells me you are a poet?"

I realised Lady Tsukii was smiling at me! I went as red as a fire engine. "Oh, no, really, really I'm not," I mumbled.

"Yes, you are," Reuben objected. "In this world."

"It would be an honour if you could compose a verse about my teahouse?" Lady Tsukii's voice was gentle, but I could tell it would be humongously rude to refuse.

"Erm, if you could just give me a moment?" I asked nervously.

I closed my eyes, and tried to remember how it felt coming out of the wintry darkness into that calm moonlit teahouse. To my relief, I came up with a poem which I can still remember:

"Your kindly light
reveals a world of hidden sorrows
glittering like frozen tears."

My poem seemed to please Lady Tsukii. She thanked me with a bow.

"I didn't mean it to come out so sad," I said apologetically.

Tsubomi looked as if she might be going to cry. "I'm very tired," she whispered.

Perhaps the lady had been burning incense in the guest room, or maybe she used some special herb to scent the quilts, because it smelled totally divine. Tsubomi and I slept on the same low futon, wrapped in fur-lined quilts. I don't know about Tsubomi, but I was as warm as a basket of kittens.

When we woke, sunlight was pouring through the blinds, and our clean, dry robes were folded neatly on the end of the futon. Lady Tsukii herself was nowhere to be seen. We replaced our slippers by the sliding door, like polite guests, and went to look for Reuben.

Tsubomi and I both burst out laughing when we saw him lolling in the natural hot pool behind the house. It did look surreal; plumes of steam rising up into the frozen trees, icicles clinking everywhere like tiny temple bells, and my angel buddy basking like a shark!

I dipped in my hand experimentally. "Eep! That's seriously hot!"

"Bliss, that's what it is, Beeby," he said lazily.

"Sorry to drag everyone away," Tsubomi said awkwardly. "But we've got to get on with this quest. I promise I'll tell you guys what it is when I know myself. I know it must seem weird."

"No probs," I said.

"It's what we're here for," said Reuben truthfully.

He hastily dried himself off and we went to find our horses.

There was still no sign of our hostess, and to be honest I wasn't that surprised. Like a magical character from a fairy tale, Lady Tsukii seemed to belong to the night and the moonlight. But our encounter with her had totally changed Tsubomi's mood for the better.

As we rode through the dazzling snowy morning, she chatted away, seeming almost like her old self; just so long as we kept it light.

Considering Tsubomi still fiercely denied she was a musician, she had v. strong opinions on the subject. It turned out she *adored* hip-hop, which pleased me (I'm the original heavenly hip-hop chick, as you know!). But if you asked her how she was so well-informed about Earth music, she said evasively, "Everyone knows this stuff, it's like, in the air."

"Sure it is, they play hip-hop constantly on Level Three," I muttered. Reuben gave me his look: like, she's getting there. Give her time.

Eventually they got into this deep conversation I couldn't make head or tail of, about silence or whatever. Reuben asked if Tsubomi had ever tried listening to silence. (I *know*! To you and me, silence means you can't hear anything, right?)

"Not just silences in music," he explained earnestly. "Any time you feel stressed, just try focusing on the gap between ordinary sounds. Say you're in a huge city with constant traffic noises, emergency sirens, pounding car radios, but you let it all wash over you, because you're just concentrating on the gap. It helps you stay calm when everyone else is stressing."

Tsubomi gave him a look of utter suspicion. "You're talking about Earth. But I don't live there. There's no stress here. It's beautiful and peaceful."

"And sad," I said softly.

"Life is sad," she said, quickly turning away.

Tsubomi didn't speak again for some time.

Towards the end of the afternoon, we came to a frozen lake, fringed with weeping willows, and spanned by a narrow footbridge.

Snow had turned the bridge into a sparkling feathery construction like you might see in a fairy tale. It looked like a bridge spun out of frozen cobwebs. On the other side was a palace of pure ice.

Tsubomi was suddenly looking pale and strained. "The Palace of Everlasting Sorrow," she whispered, as if the wind had just breathed the name in her ear. "We're going inside," she told us in a trembling voice. "There's something I have to do."

My buddy and I tethered the horses. "I think she's getting ill," I murmured.

He shook his head. "No wonder with these vibes."

As a former human, I still tend to assume that any strong emotion belongs to me. As we made our way gingerly across the cobweb bridge to the Palace of Everlasting Sorrow, painful emotions hung in the air as thickly as ice crystals. I was grateful to Reubs for reminding me that they actually belonged to Level Three.

We crunched through deep snow to the palace gates.

I'd tried to brace myself for this, but it was still distressing to see the guards standing frozen at their posts. One of them had the sweetest face. I saw Tsubomi swallow hard.

She really shouldn't be that pale, I thought.

If anything, the palace was even colder inside than out. The walls gleamed with ice, and the air was literally smoking. A vast central hall was crowded with frozen servants and lords and ladies, all fixed into rigid poses. Tsubomi's hand drifted to her face. I saw she was on the verge of fainting.

"Stay here," I told my buddy. "I'm going to find somewhere she can lie down." I was so frightened for Tsubomi I can't tell you. Every nerve ending in my body was telling me time was running out.

Yet Tsubomi was still completely adrift in a world of pure make-believe, bracing herself to battle evil ice demons, or whatever, when she simply wasn't up to it.

Tell you one thing, if I hadn't been so upset about Tsubomi, no WAY would I have had the courage to explore that palace by myself. Frozen or not, some of those Japanese noblemen were v. scary, the type who'd have you executed for, like, *sneezing* in their vicinity.

The ladies' quarter of the palace was disturbing in a different way. It was like a scene from an oriental version of Sleeping Beauty. Beautifully made-up ladies had been frozen in the middle of playing board games, untangling children's kite strings, arranging chrysanthemums, even picking their teeth! Two teenage girls were peeping shyly round a lacquered screen, just as if they'd heard me coming. I could see the rich colours of their kimonos dimly showing through the ice.

As I slid and slithered from room to icy room, I started talking angrily to myself. Well, it was more to Jessica Lightpath.

"I know you're the don of soul-retrieval, and I know we're supposed to watch and wait and it's all a totally beautiful cosmic dance and whatever, but that's for people who are already DEAD! Tsubomi's not supposed to die. Not now. Not yet. Those kids on Earth really need her, Jessica. But I don't think she can do this on her own."

Reuben found me in the state bedroom, still chatting to myself.

"Hi," he said cautiously. "Just wondered where you'd got to."

"This place is making me a bit wiggy," I explained.

He pulled a face. "I'm not surprised."

"I thought we could use this room tonight. It's

empty which is the big plus. And there's a stove. Think you can light it?"

"Hey, I'm an angel. I've been lighting fires since I was in preschool! Ask Miss Dove!"

"She must have loved you!" I called, as I flew out the door.

By the time I came back with an exhausted Tsubomi, my fire-raising angel buddy had got the stove working.

That bedroom HAD to have belonged to a princess! Everything was either gold or silver, or encrusted with pearls. OK, the bed was carved out of wood, but I bet it was v. expensive wood and it was all carved with dragons and all sorts of fabulous creatures.

Reubs and I stripped off the frozen covers, and remade the bed using two fur-lined robes instead of sheets and blankets.

Tsubomi climbed into the huge dragon bed, and turned her face to the wall, looking like a fairy-tale princess who was having a really bad day.

"Night night," I whispered, but she was already fast asleep.

I joined Reubs by the stove. Heat was pumping out, but in such a vast space it made almost no impression. We experimented with moving pretty paper screens to shut out the draft, but we were still gibbering with cold. In the end we both wrapped ourselves in Reuben's robe. It was such a relief, I can't tell you!

He gave me a mischievous look. "If this was Orlando you'd be a very happy bunny!"

"Shut up! I got over him ages ago."

"Yeah, right!"

I shook my head. "I didn't even know him, Reubs, not really. I made up this ideal boyfriend in my head and made him fit the picture."

We were sitting too close for me to see his expression.

"The first crush is the deepest," he said softly. "Isn't that what they say?"

"What about you, Mr Dark Horse?" I teased. "You never told me you'd been in love!"

Reuben sounded unusually edgy. "Who said I had?"

"You, you nutcase! We were climbing the volcano, and you said it was just like being in love."

"Oh, that!" he said in a flip voice. "That was the phoenix vibes talking. I didn't know what I was saying."

"You little devil! You don't want me to know who it is!"

"No, I don't, so drop it, Beeby." Reuben's voice had a warning vibe. He changed the subject. "Any more ideas about who's running this game?"

My buddy had virtually told me to butt out of his private life. I was SO hurt.

Typical boy, he didn't seem to notice. "I haven't smelled a whiff of a PODS since we've been here," he went on. "Have you?"

"Haven't thought about it," I snapped. "For all I know, Tsubomi's creating this entire scenario from her hospital bed."

We stared at each other.

"Omigosh," I whispered. "OMIGOSH!"

"We've got to wake her up and tell her," Reuben said.

"No way," I said firmly.

"But she thinks this is all *real*."

"Exactly. You can see how fragile she is. It could be really dangerous, like waking a sleep walker." I stiffened. "What's that?"

Tsubomi had woken from a nightmare. She was too upset to tell me what she'd dreamed about but it had clearly shaken her to the core. She cried like a little kid. "I don't know what to do, Melanie," she sobbed. "I know I'm supposed to do something really important. I just don't know what."

I held her and stroked her hair, but when someone's been sad and lonely almost her whole life, making "there, there" sounds doesn't seem like enough. I still can't explain what I did next. It's not like my singing voice has healing powers. But I did, I sang to her, I sang her a lullaby.

I seem to remember any real ones, sadly, so I just pulled soothing-sounding words out of the air, and randomly strung them together. I wasn't as embarrassed as you'd think. It felt like I was singing to myself, in a funny way, like Tsubomi and I were suddenly one person.

And it worked, that's the amazing thing. After a time, Tsubomi stopped crying altogether. She sat up in the huge dragon bed, her breath making white clouds in the air. Her eyes were full of wonder. "My father used to sing that song," she whispered.

I could feel Reuben silently sending vibes on the other side of the room. We both knew that if I did the wrong thing, Tsubomi's progress could be put back by miles.

All the same, I had to tell the truth. "He really sang that song?" I said softly. "I thought I was making it up!"

"I was scared of the dark when I was small. Dad would hear me crying and come in, and he'd raise the blind so I could see the night sky through the window. He'd say, "Don't be afraid, Mi-chan. Even on the darkest night, when we can't see her, the Moon Lady is watching over you, and he'd play his koto and sing that song."

Tsubomi sniffed back her tears. She looked around, as if she was seeing the frozen palace for the first time.

"This level isn't supposed to be ice," she said in a dismayed tone. "It's supposed to be water. I've got to change it back, and you guys have to help me."

"In the morning," I said gently. "When you've rested."

"The casket," she said urgently. "What happened to the casket?"

"It's quite safe. Look." I placed it in her hands. "Tsubomi, it's late, and this journey must have been a strain, maybe—"

"No, I have to open it now," Tsubomi insisted.

"There's something inside, which will melt the ice. I know there is!"

Reuben hurried over. "Tsubomi, we don't know for sure what's—"

She'd already raised the lid. Angry red rays were streaming into the room, touching everything with a familiar Martian glow.

I'm not sure if you were actually supposed to mix up magical objects from different levels. The phoenix egg looked ominously different on Level Three. It was *huge*, around the size of an ostrich egg, totally filling the casket. Its colours were ominous too. Hectic and much too bright, like you see on poisonous berries.

I saw Tsubomi hesitate. Before she could slam the lid, there was an ominous CRR-ACK!

When I saw that bedraggled chick trying to struggle out of its egg, I knew this wasn't going to end prettily.

OK, even phoenix demons are cute when they're babies, but this one wasn't going to be cute for much longer. The fledgling opened its beak to give a baby screech, and I saw the startling bright pink tunnel of its throat. Its eyes turned an ominous burning amber.

Oh-oh, I thought. Our sinister little cutie-pie was going to swell into a seven foot high lady demon any minute, and I knew for a fact we were all out of peach stones.

Luckily my inner angel knew exactly what to do!

"SING!" I yelled, like a character in a bad musical. "Sing like crazy!!"

"Mel, this is not the time," warned Reuben.

"It IS. Unless you want to be fried like fritters! They love music, remember?"

I started desperately warbling my moon lullaby. After the first couple of bars, the others joined in more tunefully.

"Now we're going to walk out of the palace, OK, and no one's going to make any sudden moves, and we're going to sing ALL the way."

Ever tried singing in a palace full of frozen people?

But I don't think we sounded anything like as scared as we felt. By the time we reached the bridge, the baby bird was just blissed out, blinking happily into my eyes like a hypnotised kitten.

"Tip it over the bridge," I hissed. "Quick-smart before it morphs!"

Tsubomi shut her eyes. "Sorry, sorry, sorry, little chick," she gabbled, and she upended the box.

A spark, that's all that came out!

One single gold spark, no bigger than a teeny tiny onion seed, and extraordinarily bright, as if all the fire demon's humongous power had been concentrated into one tiny spark-sized package.

Now, I'm no scientist, OK? But if you add an entire fire demon to a seriously frozen world, you can pretty much guarantee a HUGE amount of steam.

WHOOSH!!! The palace, the fairy-tale bridge, the weeping willows, instantly disappeared under a thick blanket of fog.

I groped for Tsubomi's hand. "OK, babe?"

I felt an answering squeeze.

"Reubs?"

He didn't answer.

"Reuben!" I said in a panic.

An arm came round my shoulder. "Ssh! Isn't that the loveliest sound you ever heard?"

Wasn't it just! A fabulous symphony of gurgling, trickling and splashing, as the lakes, streams, fountains and underground springs of Level Three, shook off their robes of snow and ice, and began to flow once more.

"Guys, we did it! This world is coming back to life!" Tsubomi sounded ecstatic.

YOU did it, I wanted to say. *You created the whole thing. You're STILL creating it, and I want you to stop before it's too late.*

There was a brief swirling gap in the fog, and we were all visible again. Tsubomi gave a gasp. I saw dawning realisation in her eyes. "Who *are* you guys?" she asked softly. "Omigosh, you're ang—"

But with a chime of magical music, the dripping thawing world of Level Three dissolved, and the invisible game lords sent us zooming up to the next level.

CHAPTER EIGHT

We were on the summit of a snow-capped mountain, looking down at the world far below. All of us were dressed in flowing white robes. Tsubomi's face was utterly peaceful. "If I'd known it would be like this," she said dreamily. "I wouldn't have been so scared."

This was the kind of view the old-style Japanese gods might have had; a vivid green patchwork of rice fields, little bamboo houses, streams and willows. Clouds flitted past, white and woolly as new lambs. You'd think they'd block the view, but they never did. You could see for ever, and with total god-like clarity.

If you wanted to see or hear something far away, you focused your attention, and – abracadabra! – you zoomed in for a special close-up on whatever it might be; children skimming stones across a stream, an old man snoozing in the sun, bees inside a flower. I could hear a woman singing miles below, as she stirred a pan of soup over the fire.

Reuben was standing close beside me. "You can see up as well as down." The vibration of his voice made pretty coloured trails in the air.

I looked up experimentally and got a major head rush as I zoomed in on a fizzing whizzing cosmos of stars, comets and constellations.

"Wow, this is SO cool!"

My words left pretty trails too. We'd come up through three levels, defeating demons and absorbing their energy, so according to game logic, we were now humongously powerful magicians.

Mr Allbright once told us that when we get really advanced in angelic studies, we'll actually be able to see human thoughts spreading through the Universe in ripples.

Maybe this is also true of advanced magicians? Because on Level Four, magicians seemed to be the only people around; no lute players, or ladies in wicker carriages, just pure magicians. There weren't even too many of those. Occasionally you'd spot one stalking about in the distance, looking scornful in his robes.

Level Four magicians don't tend to exert themselves unnecessarily. This is the Air level, the level of thought power. They just think themselves where they want to go, and bosh! I found it quite stressful, frowning magicians popping up among the clouds without warning.

Absolutely nothing in this world seemed fixed or solid. Houses, furniture, magic banquets, simply appeared when they were needed, and vanished when they weren't.

OK I'll own up! I *might* have been wondering about magicking myself a BLT, but Tsubomi repeated in that dreamy voice, "I didn't know it would be like this, or I wouldn't have been so scared of dying."

Reubs and I exchanged alarmed glances.

Level Four might physically resemble a small kid's idea of Heaven, high among the clouds, but it was actually a hive of v. dodgy magic.

"You're not dead, sweetie," I said firmly. "Trust me, Heaven is nothing like this." I gestured at an arrogant-looking magician, symbols glittering on his robes. "These guys are just power-tripping."

She looked as if she might burst into tears. "You're angels, I know you are! Why would I be hanging out with angels if I'm not dead?"

Trapped inside this bewildering game of changing levels and landscapes, Tsubomi badly needed something to cling to. Now I'd taken away her nice Heaven she was lost.

I had to give her courage without actually fibbing. "We were sent to help you," I told her truthfully, "with a really crucial mission."

"We did all that," said Tsubomi in a scared voice. "We stole the phoenix egg and we thawed the ice world. Is this going to go on for ever?"

I'm talking about your real mission, I wanted to say, but Reuben got in first.

"It could go on for ever, or not," he said softly. "It's up to you."

After dropping this major cosmic hint, we daren't say another word. Tsubomi would have to figure the next part out for herself.

There was a long silence. I could feel the tension build inside her.

She swallowed. "I never do anything right."

"Yeah, you do," I began.

"No, I *don't*! I can't even DIE right."

Tsubomi's words sent a storm of angry coloured lights through the air.

I was suddenly deeply scared. Was this that moment Jessica had talked about? That miraculous moment when all your watching and waiting paid off, and the human finally opened up? Because I'm sorry, it was too huge, and much too painful.

She seemed to be talking to herself. "I was too weak, that's what they said."

"Who said you were weak?" asked Reuben gently.

"Mum, Miss Kinshō. Other girls would have killed to get where I was, but I couldn't take it. Walking out on that stage night after night, dancing, singing, smiling, scared they'd see I was falling apart inside."

Tsubomi took a shaky breath.

"I was scared, I was so scared, *all* the time. It got so I couldn't eat, or sleep. I was cracking up – I was—" She shivered. "I had this crazy idea I was being stalked by things from some evil dimension."

Babe, you were, I wanted to say.

"I kept seeing these – they looked like normal pop fans, but they weren't. They weren't even real.

They'd appear out of nowhere, and stand watching me sing." She shook her head, to banish the picture. "And their *expressions* – it was like they actually wanted to destroy me. I started seeing them everywhere I went. TV studios, hotel lobbies. No one saw them but me. They wore these creepy sunglasses, but when they took them off, their—"

"Don't think about them!" I warned.

"I can't HELP it!" Tsubomi's words sent jagged lightning forks through the clouds. "Angels can control their thoughts, ordinary humans can't, OK?"

Reuben kept his voice soft and steady as if she was a scared animal. "You can decide to control them. You're a musician. Think about your music."

"I'm NOT a musician! Real musicians live and breathe music. They wouldn't do what some agent or promoter told them!"

I tried to sound calm like Reuben. "You were *young*, babe. You had no choice. You had to do what they told you. Maybe you weren't as strong as you'd like to be, but your music touches people, Tsubomi!"

"My music is total garbage!" she said in this absolutely weary voice. "I wanted to be – I wanted to touch people SO deeply. I guess I just don't have what it takes."

I'd never been so terrified for Tsubomi as I was then. In a world of magicians, just thinking about something would make it true. If Tsubomi thought she was too weak to fight, she was. If she thought her life had been pointless, it was.

This was the moment the Dark Powers had been banking on; the moment of unbearable loneliness and despair which would destroy all final hopes of Tsubomi returning to complete her Agency mission.

She swallowed. "Have you ever heard my first record? I'm just a fake. You guys have been great, but you should go back to Heaven now and stop wasting your time on fakes and losers."

Her magician's robes were melting away as she spoke. Underneath she wore the normal teenage uniform of the twenty-first century: jeans, trainers and a hoodie. She pulled the hood over her shiny dark hair, and trudged off across the clouds.

Somewhere in a viewing suite in the Hell dimensions, PODS agents were howling in triumph and stomping their feet.

The battle for Tsubomi's soul was over. They'd won.

In that terrible moment, I felt myself split into three angels. One watched Tsubomi walk away, totally convinced that everything was lost. A second angel stood sorrowfully beside a hospital bed where a dying girl was just about to be unplugged from a life-support machine.

The third angel knew it was time for Tsubomi to know the truth.

I made my robes dissolve too. I'd had enough of disguises.

"Mi-chan!" I called, deliberately using her family pet name. "Don't you want to know who's doing this to you?"

There was no expression in Tsubomi's face. "Does it even matter?"

"You're going to die, girl," I told her softly. "You at least owe it to yourself to ask where this has all been coming from; all these phoenix eggs and frozen palaces and talking mice!"

I saw her throat muscles move. Her eyes went wide. "NO way. Are you *crazy*! I don't have that kind of power."

"Tsubomi, you have so much power you're scaring yourself. You created an entire magic world out of your imagination, using stuff you remembered from video games, fairy tales you heard as a little kid, like those little dead Limbo children, and the Moon Lady."

She shook her head. "I don't believe you. Why would I do that?"

"I don't know why, babe. Maybe you just wanted to hide inside a fairy tale for a while? Or maybe you were using it to make yourself stronger, so you could go back to Earth and stand up to the Dark Powers. But I know one thing. You're pure magic, Tsubomi. You've just got to learn to control it, that's all."

She looked dazed, like someone on the verge of waking from a long, confusing dream. "It's just a stupid game, none of it's real."

"It IS. In a way it is!" I gestured at the rice fields far below. "This came out of you, Tsubomi. All this incredible beauty is you!"

I could see Tsubomi longed to believe me, but she didn't dare. She just didn't dare.

Reuben has the best cosmic timing of any angel I know.

"Won't you play for us one last time before you go?" he asked slyly.

She tried to smile. "Maybe you didn't notice, but I haven't got an instrument."

Ruben casually materialised a stunningly beautiful koto. Painted on the sides in gold leaf were Japanese characters for all the elements that make up the Universe: Earth, Fire, Water and Air.

Tsubomi backed away. "It's only got one string."

My angel buddy firmly pushed her towards the instrument. "You heard Lady Tsukii. Harp players have played with one string before."

"Not many. Only a master could play that well."

"So play, Tsubomi!" Reuben almost whispered.

That's when he gave her his special Sweetpea smile. Who would believe that an angel's smile could totally tip the balance between Light and Darkness?

Yet in that moment I could see Tsubomi believed him.

She was shaking, but she seated herself cross-legged in front of the koto, shut her eyes and began to play. Even now, just thinking about it, gives me goose bumps. From that single string, this amazing girl produced the most exquisite rhythms and harmonies I have ever heard outside Heaven.

At one point the people who lived at the bottom of the mountain fell silent in awe. Maybe they thought they could hear the music of the gods?

Reuben and Tsubomi were so deeply into the music that they both had their eyes closed, so I was the only one who saw the landscape dissolve for the fifth and final time.

We were back where we'd started, only everything had changed. Level One was going totally potty, putting out bright green shoots and teeny little flower buds.

Music was playing somewhere among the trees: drums, flutes and biwas. Some kind of festival was going on.

Crowds of beautifully dressed little girls were walking about under blossoming peach and cherry trees, proudly dressed in their new spring kimonos. They had that genuine dignity little kids have on important occasions, but you could see their eyes sparkling with fun.

Some had dressed their dolls in *their* spring kimonos, and brought them out to share the celebrations. Others were flying kites shaped like fabulous birds and beasts. At one shrine, little girls were busy writing their secret wishes on slips of paper and tying them to flowering branches with coloured ribbons.

When you've just been fighting for someone's soul, it's a little overwhelming to find yourself surrounded by a sea of zingy blossomy springtime vibes.

Tsubomi took our hands. "What can I say? I was a goner and you just pulled me back out of the dark."

Reuben grinned. "Just doin' our job, ma-am!"

Girls often feel they have to hide parts of themselves that don't fit, don't they? They think they should be the same as everyone else, or they think they should be perfect. But when I looked into Tsubomi's eyes, I knew she wasn't going to be hiding any more.

You know how it is when you say goodbye to someone you probably won't see again for some time? You've only got like, *minutes*, so you frantically try to fit in everything you really meant to say earlier if you'd only had time.

"So really you were right about being on a quest," my inner angel was telling Tsubomi earnestly. "But this one's on Earth, so it's probably pretty much going to take your whole life."

"And the Dark Powers come in all kinds of disguises, so you won't always recognise them right off," my buddy chipped in equally earnestly.

"It'll be harsh sometimes. People won't always understand what you or your music are about, and some days you'll feel like you're all alone in a huge meaningless Universe."

"Yeah yeah, Auntie, and I'll eat all my vegetables and I promise I won't talk to strangers!" she teased.

"But you're *not* alone," I went on fiercely. "You're NEVER alone. Everything and everyone in this Universe is—"

Reuben nudged me. "I think it's time for her to go," he whispered.

I saw a familiar figure strolling towards us. He was not only *much* less hairy, the hermit also looked decades younger, and far more twinkly than the first time we met him. Awed little girls bowed their heads reverently on either side, like flowers in a meadow. They knew what I'd only just realised. Our hermit was Jizo, the kindly children's god who refuses to enter the Pure Land until every lost soul is safe inside.

He looked into Tsubomi's eyes and smiled.

"Are you ready to go back?"

Tsubomi nodded. "Yes." She gave us a sudden beseeching look. "Will I see you again?"

"For sure," Reuben promised.

"And remember, babe," I called, "everything in the Universe is—"

The god and the teenage pop star were swallowed in a blaze of golden light.

"—connected," I whispered.

CHAPTER NINE

"I don't understand why you feel so bad. You guys totally saved her from being rubbed out by the PODS. You should be over the moon!"

To my relief, Lola had totally forgiven me. Her eyes were dark with sympathy.

"I am over the moon, mostly, it's just..." I tried to put my feelings into words. "I know Tsubomi's really talented and everything, but deep down she's just like we were, Lollie. She's pure magic, a real undercover angel. And she's had to cope with all this stuff."

Lola took a sip of her smoothie. "It's not easy growing up magic on planet Earth."

"That's why I wish I'd helped her more."

Lola and I were sitting at a pavement table, outside Guru, our fave student café. We'd been there since they opened; working our way through their yummy celestial breakfast special, ordering a succession of smoothies and talking.

"I just feel like I missed such a valuable opportunity," I said wistfully. "If you have an encounter with angels, you should come out of it knowing all this, like, totally luminous stuff, right? Reuben was great with her, telling her how to deal with stress and whatever. She'll remember that next time, I know she will."

"You must have talked to her too?"

"Yeah, about hip-hop," I sighed. "Oh, and we had a heated discussion about whether combats are on the way out."

"NO way," said Lola fiercely.

I grinned. "Exactly what I said."

"So what would you have told her, hon?"

"You know, all that stuff that trainee angels take for granted. Like those cosmic strings Mr Allbright was telling us about the other day."

Lola looked amazed. "Strings? Was I away that lesson?"

"OK, maybe they're not actually strings. Maybe it's more like an energy grid."

"An *energy* grid?" Lola seemed to be in severe physical pain.

"OK, scrub the grid. Stick with the string. Imagine there's a HUGE game of cat's cradle, but the strings are so fine and so closely interwoven it's like this big shimmery mesh."

My soul-mate frowned. "How big?"

"Sorry, didn't I say? It's exactly the same size as the cosmos, duh! Forgot that bit!"

"It's OK, I've got it now. Shimmery strings forming a humongous cosmic cat's cradle. Now what?"

"Ah, but they're not really strings, you see," I explained patiently. "It's more like a net made out of incredibly subtle cosmic energy. Mr Allbright says ancient Hindus knew all about it, but humans don't usually see it, unless they're like, *massively* spiritual."

"Or smoking something they shouldn't," Lola grinned. "So what does it do, this shimmery energy net that no one's seen and I've totally never heard of?"

"Don't mock the net, girlfriend, this net is really, really, cool. It's like this live shimmery information system, that connects absolutely everything and everyone to everyone and everything else."

Lola frowned. "Info literally goes whizzing down the strings – like, even between Heaven and Earth and whatever?"

I nodded. "All those times on Earth, when you knew something you couldn't possibly have known! You just downloaded it from the energy net, without realising!"

Lola was genuinely impressed. "Hey that IS cool! That explains so much!"

"I know. Like the guy in the record store 'accidentally' giving me that Japanese harp CD, like, *hours* before I go to save a girl whose dad makes Japanese harps."

"So how does it work?" she asked abruptly.

"I knew you were going to ask me that," I wailed. "Look, I totally understood it when Mr Allbright explained it, OK?"

Lola tactfully helped me to three more pancakes. "Have you heard how Tsubomi's getting on these days? Is she OK?"

"According to Sam, she's back in school and living with her dad." I took a big bite of pancake.

Lola's eyes went huge. "You guys went through all that and then she *gave up* singing!"

"No, sorry, sorry," I said with my mouth full. "Tsubomi's just dropped the touring and the promotional stuff. Sam says she's focusing on her song-writing for now. She's putting some amazing album together." I gave Lola a meaningful look. "Apparently it was inspired by some experiences she had during her illness."

"Oh, wow, just imagine *that* video," Lola said enviously.

Glossy MTV images flitted through my mind. The pale underworld princess being tempted by a bowl of mouth-watering strawberries. An action princess in sexy ninja costume, abseiling over a moat of lava to steal a phoenix egg from a fire demon. A lonely lost princess in an ice palace full of frozen lords and ladies, one cold crystal tear sliding down her cheek.

Lola looked dreamy. "I wonder who they'll get to play you and Reubs?"

I sighed. "I miss her, Lollie. I know I'm going on and on about it, but it was the most amazing mission."

"It must have been. Reuben's just the same." She gave me a sideways glance. "You and he got quite close on this trip, right?"

"We've always been close," I said in surprise. "It was just really special to be able to share the experience with a friend."

"Sure," she said hastily. "Hey, it was your last mission. A last mission is supposed to be fabulous. I'm glad, honestly." Lola couldn't seem to meet my eyes.

"Omigosh! I can't believe I didn't tell you! I'm not quitting."

Pure relief dawned in her eyes. "You're *not*? You're REALLY not?"

I patted her hand. "I'm really not. I lost it for a bit, that's all. I think I was kind of burned out. Ancient Rome, Brice's mission to Jamaica—"

"—your best friend getting cosmic amnesia," Lola said softly.

"All that," I agreed. "I'd let everything get on top of me. I guess I needed a break."

My mate shook her head. "Sorry, chasing a confused soul through a Limbo dimension isn't my idea of a picnic in the park."

"OK, it wasn't exactly a picnic, but it was different to anything I'd ever done before, and in a funny way it helped me get my confidence back. I found all these other aspects of me I didn't even know I had. I could fight like a ninja. Can you believe I was actually making up all this v. deep poetry! Like, right there on the spot!"

I took a deep breath. "I'm not ready to hang up my combats, Lollie. I want to go on fighting the PODS with you guys."

"And this is really what you want? It's not because I threw a Sanchez-sized tantrum?" Lola looked guilty.

"No way, hon! It's more like I can't stand to think of you all going off and having thrilling adventures without me!"

Lola produced a gift-wrapped package and pushed it across the table.

"What's this?" I said in surprise. "My birthday isn't for weeks."

"I know that, but I thought you were giving up trouble-shooting, *carita*. I wanted to give you a pressie, to show my support for your stupid wrong-headed decision."

I unwrapped the layers of spangly bright pink tissue.

"Ohh, Lola, that is the most darling thing!"

My mate had made me a photo frame, and decorated it with heavenly love hearts! Each heart had a cute message like, "Celestial Chick", or "No Angel"! Inside was a mad picture Brice had taken of Lola, me and Reuben on a school field trip.

"Yeah, well totally pointless gesture as it turns out," Lola said grumpily.

"I love it, Lollie, thanks SO much!"

I smiled down at our three laughing faces in their frame. Reuben can look really daffy in photos, but Brice had managed to catch him off guard. *That boy is something else,* I thought. *How did he even know to smile at Tsubomi at that precise moment?* Reuben had all these hidden depths that I'd never remotely suspected. I could see why Tanya fancied him. I could almost have fancied him myself, you know. If he wasn't a good mate.

I carefully rewrapped the photo frame. I wondered if Lola had heard anything about our buddy's mysterious love interest?

I was just about to pump her for info, when my soul-mate came out with a mind-blowing suggestion.

"You could put it in a book," she mumbled through her pancake.

I was lost. "Put what in a book, babe?"

"All that crucial cosmic information you didn't get a chance to tell her. You could write an unofficial cosmic handbook for kids like Tsubomi. Hey, forget humans, *I'd* use it! The one the school gives out is really heavy going. I zonk out after about half a chapter."

"I've read like two chapters since I've been here," I confessed.

Lola beamed. "My point exactly. The Universe *needs* your handbook, Boo. You should definitely do it."

I found myself getting cautiously excited.

"I'd have to write it how I talk."

"Kids would LOVE that! You could tell them about that shimmery net and how everything is connected and how the Universe always has to answer when you call."

"We'd have to tell them the dark stuff too," I said.

Lola nodded eagerly. "Totally, it would be like, a survival guide for undercover angels who have to live on Earth."

"Lollie, that's the most completely luminous idea! I couldn't do it on my own, though. You'd help me, right?" I asked anxiously.

Lola seemed wistful suddenly.

"What's the matter, hon?"

She sighed. "I know cosmic timing is always perfect, but I just can't help wishing someone could have thought of it before. A book like that could have made all the difference to me when I was alive."

"Me too," I said softly. "Oh, totally, babe, me too."

STOP PRESS!

COSMICALLY MIND-BLOWING NEWS!
We, that's me and Lollie, have started a newsletter:

COSMIC BUZZ!

Subscribe now and we'll send you all the hot goss,
including the Heavenly Top Ten; the coolest beats
reverberating in Heaven; gourmet Guru food; celestial
recipes to share; super-sparkly fashion tips; hair tricks
straight from the Academy and even sneaky peeks
into our secret, special diaries. Also, don't miss the
chance to win some completely divine prizes!

To subscribe just log on to
www.angelsunlimited.co.uk

Get all the fab news on looking good, feeling good
and having a totally luminous time – straight from the
chic-est chicks in Heaven!

Love, Mel Beeby
a.k.a. the trouble-shooting, trouble-making angel!

Order Form

To order direct from the publishers, just make a list of the titles you want and fill in the form below:

Name ....

Address ....

....

....

Send to: Dept 6, HarperCollins Publishers Ltd, Westerhill Road, Bishopbriggs, Glasgow G64 2QT.

Please enclose a cheque or postal order to the value of the cover price, plus:

UK & BFPO: Add £1.00 for the first book, and 25p per copy for each additional book ordered.

Overseas and Eire: Add £2.95 service charge. Books will be sent by surface mail but quotes for airmail despatch will be given on request.

A 24-hour telephone ordering service is available to holders of Visa, MasterCard, Amex or Switch cards on 0141- 772 2281.

An imprint of HarperCollinsPublishers